THE WHISPERING CRYPT

A DARK ARCHAEOLOGY SHORT STORY

ERNEST DEMPSEY

138 PUBLISHING

1

Tariq froze. A sudden, icy dread clamped down on his chest, stilling the very air in his lungs. He knew they shouldn't be here, shouldn't be trespassing in this place. He'd said as much to the lead archaeologist on the project. It didn't matter their crew had permission to be there excavating. The dead give permission to no one.

The light behind him flickered as the generator hummed several meters back. Its monotonous drone was a constant, mechanical heartbeat against the tomb's ancient silence, a sound that felt profoundly out of place. Extension cords stretched like roots across the sand-packed floor, leading deeper into the corridor, where halogen lamps on steel tripods washed the stone walls in pale white.

They had discovered the stairway three weeks ago—an angled shaft hidden beneath layers of collapsed masonry near the back of the temple site. At first, Dr. El-Amin believed it was nothing more than a service passage. But as they dug, the stairs kept going. Twenty steps. Then thirty. Then forty. By the time they reached the bottom, they found themselves facing a corridor carved directly into bedrock, untouched by modern tools.

No one had seen what lay beyond this hallway in over four thousand years.

The air inside was dry and oddly still. No insects. No whiff of rot or mildew. It wasn't the freshness of preservation, it was the kind of silence that felt deliberate, as if the passage had been sealed not just physically, but spiritually.

Dr. Hatem El-Amin walked ahead now, his shoulders hunched beneath his khaki field jacket. His hands were stuffed into his pockets, not from the chill—it was sweltering even down here—but from habit. Nerves. Tariq had seen that same telltale sign before at the Giza incident, a subtle tension in the professor's jaw that betrayed a mind wrestling with something it couldn't yet define. This wasn't his first tomb. He had spent his life studying Old Kingdom necropolises and supervising excavations across the Saqqara Plateau. But this one had unsettled him from the beginning.

The corridor sloped gently downward, the walls cut with unusual precision. It was a level of craftsmanship that spoke not of simple labor, but of a deep, almost fanatical devotion to the task, making the complete lack of decoration even more unnerving. Not a single pictograph or ceremonial etching marked the sandstone—until the final ten meters.

That was where the symbols began.

Tariq had photographed them, catalogued them, and tried to cross-reference them using the university's image database. A few matched standard hieroglyphs. One was the unmistakable glyph for "death"—a half circle atop a vertical slash, unmistakable even to a student. But others were stranger, more abstract. Spirals. Interlocking crescents. One symbol resembled a human eye fractured by horizontal lines, like static etched into stone. None of them had appeared in their records. It was the professional equivalent of finding a sentence written in a language that had never existed; a chilling impossibility.

El-Amin had said little since they reached the sealed door two days ago. He spent most of his time staring at it in silence, running gloved fingers across the seams, and pacing between light stands. He took no photos. Refused to take samples. Refused to allow anyone else to, either.

Now, as Tariq caught up to him, they stood before the stone door once more.

It stood taller than a man, carved from a single slab of granite. Faint veins of quartz ran through it like frozen lightning. Unlike the clean walls of the passage, the door was covered in symbols—etched not with care, but with urgency. As if someone had carved them in haste, or desperation.

The central glyph for death sat directly at eye level.

Tariq swallowed. His shirt clung to his back.

El-Amin exhaled through his nose, then nodded to the two assistants behind them—local laborers who had helped carry the electric winch equipment down into the corridor earlier that morning. Tariq heard the metallic click of cables being locked into place.

"Whatever is in there hasn't been seen by human eyes for thousands of years," El-Amin said, his voice barely above a whisper.

Tariq looked at the door again. Something about it felt... aware.

Dr. El-Amin stepped away from the door, nodding to the two workers as he did. The men responded wordlessly, each moving with careful precision toward the equipment they had set in place earlier that morning. Tariq watched them feed the final cable through the pulley anchor bolted into the corridor floor, then secure it to the heavy steel bracket clamped to the left edge of the stone slab.

The corridor felt smaller now.

The air, dry just moments before, had taken on a weight. It settled in the lungs and refused to leave, like they were breathing the inside of a tomb already opened.

El-Amin spoke quietly. "Once it starts moving, stay back. The seal may give all at once."

Tariq nodded, his throat tight. He stepped behind the first row of lights, joining the doctor at a safer distance. The tripods cast tall shadows against the stone as the winch motor engaged with a mechanical click.

The generator groaned louder behind them on the surface above.

With a signal from one of the men, the winch began its slow pull. At first, nothing happened. The thick cable drew taut, the bracket straining against the stubborn granite. The corridor echoed with a low mechanical hum.

Then came a sound none of them expected. A sharp crack, like stone splintering under pressure. The sound was shockingly violent in the confined space, echoing down the corridor like a bone snapping.

Tariq flinched. Dust trickled down from the ceiling. A second later, a hairline gap appeared between the door and its frame— barely wide enough to slip a blade through, but enough to prove it was moving.

"Steady," El-Amin warned, his voice nearly drowned out by the sound of the generator's motor.

The winch slowed as the resistance increased. Stone groaned against stone, the grinding noise deep and unpleasant, like the sound of distant thunder held too long. Every centimeter seemed to take an eternity. Sweat slid unnoticed down Tariq's neck. He could hear his own heartbeat over the machinery.

Another inch. Then two.

The seal cracked in another place, higher up this time. A faint hissing sound escaped the gap, followed by a wave of cold, dry air. Not foul, not wet—just ancient. It was an air devoid of life, carrying no scent of decay or moisture, only the sterile, mineral tang of time itself. It carried no smell, but it made the skin crawl.

Tariq's gaze locked on the opening. A darkness stared back. Not the absence of light, but something thicker. Something that refused to be lit.

The winch operator adjusted the tension again. The gap widened to the width of a hand.

One of the workers muttered a prayer under his breath.

"Stop it there," El-Amin said suddenly.

The men obeyed, switching off the winch. The motor whined down to an idle. Tariq stepped forward, then he stopped, and allowed El-Amin to pass.

The archaeologist leaned forward, peering into the cavity. He pointed a flashlight into the opening, and tilted his head. Hidden behind the stone slab was not a room, not immediately, just more darkness and flat walls. Dust motes hung in still air as if frozen in time.

And something else. Carvings. Not like the ones on the outside. These were deeper. Sharper. Etched into the interior walls just beyond the threshold, and catching the light in strange, fractured patterns.

"Tariq," El-Amin called, voice low but firm.

Tariq met the man's eyes.

He looked at the others. "We go in together. But only once we've documented the entrance fully. No one crosses this threshold until we know what we're dealing with."

The corridor remained silent.

Behind the half-open door, the darkness waited.

Dr. El-Amin lowered his flashlight. The beam had reached only a few meters into the darkness beyond the gap before dissolving into the dust. He hadn't liked what he saw—or more accurately, what he couldn't see.

He turned back to the winch team. "Resume the pull. Slowly. Keep it steady."

The older of the two workers gave a single nod. The younger man glanced at the gap, then busied himself checking the anchor bolts once more. Neither spoke.

Tariq took a half-step backward, feeling the tension return to the air. It pressed against his chest like the weight of the corridor itself had shifted. He didn't want to admit it, but he felt something watching from beyond that crack in the stone.

The motor kicked on again, vibrating through the floor. Steel cables strained and groaned as the winch resumed its work, drawing the massive door with aching reluctance.

Dust peeled from the edges of the granite slab as it moved. Not in a rush, but in slow, deliberate resistance, like a hand being forced open finger by finger.

Tariq kept his eyes on the widening gap. As it grew, the space beyond began to take shape. The interior chamber was taller than expected, with walls that angled upward at sharp, almost architectural slopes. Not the smooth curves of a burial chamber. Not the standard design of any dynasty he had studied.

A rush of colder air slid out past them, brushing Tariq's face like a whisper. It smelled of minerals and something older. To him, it felt like something not meant to be disturbed.

The door shifted another half meter. The winch whined in protest. A low shriek of metal scraped across stone, followed by a sudden drop in resistance. The slab jerked slightly and then rolled free with a final shuddering drag, settling just beyond the carved threshold.

The noise ceased, and the silence fell hard through the tunnel. No wind. No echo. Even the generator's distant hum seemed muffled now, swallowed by the breathless stillness of the newly opened chamber.

Tariq stared into it. It wasn't just dark. It was wrong. The light didn't behave as it should. The far wall absorbed it without reflection, making the space seem endless even though it clearly wasn't. And those carvings—dozens of them—covered every surface of the inner walls. Some mirrored the symbols from the outer corridor, but others were unfamiliar, aggressive in shape and depth. Symbols that did not belong to any recorded script.

Dr. El-Amin stepped forward, stopping just short of the entrance. He raised his flashlight again, slowly scanning the interior.

"We go in slowly," he said. "You all know the rules. No one touches anything. Photograph every surface. Log every symbol. And stay together."

The two workers exchanged a look. Tariq said nothing, but his fingers itched at his sides. Something inside him knew they had crossed a line just by opening the way.

They had forced an answer to a question no one should have asked. Behind the now-silent winch, the stone slab rested against the far wall like a fallen sentinel. And before them, the chamber waited.

Tariq stepped across the threshold.

The air inside the chamber felt different from the corridor. Not colder, exactly, but thicker—like breathing through fabric. Every inhalation was an effort, the atmosphere dense and heavy, as if saturated with an unseen presence. His boots pressed into a layer of dust so fine it barely stirred beneath his weight. It had settled here for centuries without disturbance. No footprints. No tool marks. No rodent trails or signs of life.

This place had not been opened before.

The others followed. Dr. El-Amin came next, his flashlight beam sweeping across the angular walls. The two workers entered last, their footsteps hesitant, wide eyes scanning the walls as if they expected them to move.

The chamber was roughly rectangular, longer than it was wide, with a slightly sloping ceiling that tapered into a low ridge above them. The walls had been carved with care, but it was the markings that drew immediate attention.

Hieroglyphs stretched from floor to ceiling in uneven, chaotic bands.

Some were familiar. Tariq recognized symbols he'd seen countless times—royal titles, funerary rites, invocations to the gods of the underworld. But others were not Egyptian at all. Some looked like glyphs, but were constructed from sharp, repeating angles. Others curved in looping patterns that reminded him of the markings on the coils of an old radio.

A strange hum settled behind his ears. It wasn't audible, not exactly, but present. He rubbed his jaw and tried to shake it off.

"There," El-Amin said, his voice low. He pointed toward the back of the chamber.

The sarcophagus stood alone against the far wall.

It was massive—longer than any standard design, with sharp corners and a heavy lid flush with the base. Its sheer scale was a statement of importance, or perhaps of warning, dominating the chamber by its very existence. It was made of dark stone, not black but greenish, like serpentine rock, streaked with veins of gray. There were no handles. No latches. No seals.

Just stone. And like the walls, its surface was carved.

El-Amin approached slowly, careful not to let his light linger on any one area too long. He reached into his coat and pulled out a small notepad, flipping it open.

"These symbols," he said, gesturing toward a panel near the head of the sarcophagus, "are unmistakably Egyptian. Old Kingdom dialect."

He read slowly, lips barely moving.

"This one here... says 'condemned.' And here—'no honor in death.' This is unusual. Most sarcophagi celebrate the life of the deceased. This speaks only of punishment."

Tariq looked closer. "What does that one mean?"

El-Amin followed his finger. "'He betrayed the divine order.'"

The doctor stepped to the other side. His eyes moved across another column of hieroglyphs, slower now. "This... this is a warning."

He ran his fingers gently over the carvings. "'Let none disturb the one within. For his voice brings the end of memory. His name is silence. His hunger is thought. If you open this tomb, the curse shall pass not into the world, but into the mind of the world.'"

He stopped reading. El-Amin fell silent, the final words hanging in the dead air, their meaning both cryptic and terrifyingly specific. No one spoke.

Tariq glanced at the strange symbols woven between the Egyptian ones. They didn't match any script he knew. He had seen fragments of other proto-languages—early Mesopotamian, pre-dynastic pictographs, even some Cycladic etchings—but nothing like this.

"These others," he said, "what language are they?"

El-Amin didn't answer at first.

Finally, he said, "They're not a language I recognize."

"Could they be a code?"

"Or something older."

The two workers stood near the entrance, whispering to each

other in nervous Arabic. Tariq couldn't hear the words, but he could feel their meaning. This place wasn't like the others.

It didn't feel buried. It felt sealed. As if the purpose of the tomb had never been to honor the dead... but to keep something in.

Dr. El-Amin knelt beside the sarcophagus, notebook resting against one thigh, pencil moving slowly. The beam of his flashlight angled upward from a tripod behind him, casting his shadow long and narrow across the far wall.

"Photograph everything," he said. "Start on the east wall, move left to right. No flashes. Use side light to capture the engravings."

Tariq nodded, already adjusting the LED panel on the camera rig. The corridor's halogen bulbs didn't reach this far into the chamber, so every detail had to be caught by hand. He knelt beside the first band of symbols, some of which looped and spiraled in ways that seemed to evade logic. One glyph reminded him of an ouroboros, but fractured, its circle broken at three points. He pressed the shutter. The click echoed louder than it should have.

Tariq glanced over his shoulder, but the others hadn't reacted. The two workers were tracing the perimeter of the chamber with chalk markers, identifying areas for later scans. Dr. El-Amin remained focused on the sarcophagus, murmuring translations to himself as he worked.

Tariq turned back to the wall. His breath caught. The camera display showed a symbol he hadn't seen before—one just to the left of the one he had photographed. A sharp-angled spiral with spines radiating outward like thorns. He leaned in. There was no such carving on the wall in front of him. The stone was blank in that spot. He looked back to the display. The symbol remained. His mind scrambled for a logical explanation. A glitch in the camera's software? A trick of the light reflecting off crystalline particles in the stone? But he knew, with a certainty that chilled him to the bone, that he had captured something that wasn't there.

He lowered the camera and stood. The hair on his arms rose, though the air remained still. He took another photo, same angle, same lighting. This time, the symbol wasn't there. He checked the previous image again. Still visible.

Behind him, El-Amin spoke, his voice low but edged. "Something's wrong with the light."

Tariq turned. The flashlight beam had begun to flicker, subtly at first, then with a regular pulse. Not a loss of power, but a rhythm. Almost like breathing. Then it steadied again, perfectly bright.

The workers had stopped what they were doing. One of them stepped back toward the corridor.

El-Amin rose slowly; eyes fixed on the flashlight.

"It's not the generator," he said. "The corridor lights are steady. It's just this one."

He crossed the chamber and tapped the housing. No loose connection. He picked it up and angled it toward the walls, then the sarcophagus. The beam didn't falter.

But the moment he set it back on the tripod and turned away, the flickering resumed.

Tariq swallowed. "Could it be a vibration in the floor?"

"No," El-Amin said. "The tripod's rubber mounted."

He stepped back again, still watching the light. "It stopped."

Tariq tried to speak, but hesitated. Instead, he opened the camera's gallery and quietly deleted the photo that didn't match what was real. It felt wrong to keep it. Like preserving something that wasn't supposed to exist.

He turned back to the wall. Now the symbol was there. Cut into the stone as if it always had been.

Tariq stared at it, frozen. The lines were etched deep. Fresh. He reached out and touched the grooves with two fingers. He stepped back, chest tightening.

"Professor?" he said.

The doctor turned. Tariq pointed to the glyph.

"This wasn't here before."

El-Amin approached, studying the carving without touching it. "You're sure?"

"I took a photo. It wasn't there. Then it was only on the screen. Then it was... here."

He waited for the doctor to laugh, or scold him, or explain it away. But El-Amin only stared.

"We document it," he said finally. "Nothing more." He turned back toward the sarcophagus, but his steps were slower now. More careful.

As if he, too, had begun to wonder whether they had already triggered something.

Tariq crouched beside the eastern wall, pencil and notepad in hand, copying a cluster of the smaller, unfamiliar symbols into his logbook. He worked quietly, tuning out the faint hum of the generator behind him and the low rustle of chalk as Mahmoud and Karim continued marking the grid layout on the floor.

Dr. El-Amin moved slowly around the sarcophagus, photographing the carvings with his personal camera. He spoke occasionally into his voice recorder, noting the pattern of the warnings, the layering of languages, the anomalous syntax. The tension that had haunted the earlier hours seemed to have dulled. They were working again. Focused and professional.

"We'll want full rubbings of the lid," El-Amin said, his voice echoing slightly. "Every surface. If these inscriptions are meant as containment... they may form a pattern."

"I'll start with the base," Tariq replied.

He removed a roll of parchment-thin transfer paper from his satchel and began pressing it gently against the side of the sarcophagus. The surface was cool, the grooves beneath the paper sharp and angular. He smoothed the sheet flat with gloved hands, then began rubbing with charcoal, slow circles revealing the etched forms beneath.

At first, they appeared normal—at least as normal as anything here could be. But halfway across the panel, the charcoal darkened over an area with no discernible symbol. The pattern looked like interference—jagged and incomplete.

Tariq paused. He lifted the paper to check the stone itself.

Nothing.

That section of the sarcophagus was smooth. No carving at all. But the pattern had transferred onto the rubbing.

He stared at it, heart ticking faster.

Behind him, Mahmoud was muttering to himself. Tariq glanced over.

The worker had stopped drawing. He stood facing the corner of the chamber, head tilted slightly. His shoulders were rigid, arms at his sides, chalk still clutched in one hand.

Tariq called his name. "Mahmoud?"

No answer.

Karim, crouched nearby, looked up too. "He's doing it again," he whispered.

Dr. El-Amin approached from the far side of the sarcophagus. "What's wrong with him?"

Tariq stood. "I don't know. He was fine just a moment ago."

El-Amin stepped closer. "Mahmoud."

The man turned slowly.

His lips were moving, but the words were faint. Repetitive. Not Arabic. Not Coptic. Not anything Tariq recognized.

It wasn't until El-Amin stepped closer that the sound shifted.

The acoustics of the chamber changed—subtly but unmistakably. Like a filter had been placed over everything. The high frequencies vanished. Footsteps no longer echoed. The sound of breath became sharper, closer, like the walls had moved in.

"Stop," El-Amin said firmly. "Everyone stop what you're doing."

Tariq froze.

Karim rose slowly, brushing dust from his knees.

Mahmoud blinked hard, as if waking from sleep. He looked around, confused and disoriented. His jaw trembled slightly, and he stumbled back a step.

"I heard…" he began, then stopped.

El-Amin turned to Tariq. "What were you doing just before this?"

"I took a rubbing from the side. That's all."

"Show me."

Tariq handed him the paper. The doctor studied it carefully. His brow tightened.

"This symbol... it's not on the stone?"

"No. It appeared only on the rubbing."

El-Amin said nothing for a long moment.

Then he folded the paper in half, slowly and precisely, and tucked it into his notebook.

"We're leaving," he said.

Mahmoud pressed his palms tightly to his temples. Karim stepped toward him, hesitating.

"We'll reseal the door," El-Amin continued. "If we're right... if the function of this place is containment, we may have already broken something."

The lights flickered.

Only once.

But it was enough to confirm what they all now felt. Something in this tomb was wrong. Very wrong.

Dr. El-Amin moved fast now, faster than he had all day. His voice, sharp and urgent, cut through the thickening silence of the chamber.

"Wrap the equipment. We need to get out of here."

Karim dropped his chalk and turned toward the corridor. Mahmoud didn't move.

Tariq stood rooted to the spot. Something trembled deep within his soul. His face remained calm and expressionless; too calm.

"Tariq," El-Amin called.

He didn't answer.

The lights flickered again, longer this time, but not like before. This was rhythmic; like a stutter. The generator's hum outside the chamber faltered, then surged.

Mahmoud began to shake.

At first it was subtle—his shoulders twitching, his breath catching in stutters—but then he dropped to his knees. His head tipped back and a low groan spilled from his throat; not pained, but mechanical and repetitive.

El-Amin rushed toward him. "Karim, help me."

They reached Mahmoud as he began to speak.

Not Arabic. Not English.

The voice that came out was flat and distorted, broken by static that didn't exist in the room. It was a horrifying auditory illusion; a sound layered over reality that seemed to emanate directly from the air itself.

Words tumbled out in a dialect none of them recognized. Some were choked with phlegm, others perfectly enunciated, but none of it belonged to him.

Tariq tilted his head as if listening.

"Don't... look at him," El-Amin said, turning to Karim. "Get back to the corridor."

But Karim was staring.

Tears streamed from his eyes. His lips moved, silently at first, then utterances echoing Mahmoud's syllables, just half a beat behind. Not mimicry, but in sync.

El-Amin dragged Mahmoud away from the wall. The man was trembling violently now, hands clutching the floor, blood trickling from one nostril. His eyes were open, but no longer blinking.

"Tariq, move," El-Amin shouted.

Tariq finally looked at him.

His face was blank. Too blank. Like something had paused behind his skin.

"I understand now," he said softly.

El-Amin froze.

"I know what it means," Tariq continued. "The glyph. The voice. It's not a language. It's a function. A command."

Behind him, the sarcophagus gave off a soft, groaning sound. Stone on stone.

The lid hadn't moved.

But the dust along its edge was shifting—inward, as if pulled by breath.

El-Amin stood and grabbed Tariq by the shoulder. "We have to go."

Tariq turned slowly. "It's already happening."

Karim let out a short, sharp scream behind them as he collapsed onto his side, seizing. Mahmoud slumped forward, his breath gone, still muttering with lips that no longer moved.

El-Amin pulled Tariq by force.

They staggered toward the corridor.

The chamber behind them pulsed again; once, deep and low, not a sound but a pressure. The electric lights burst in a pop of glass. The generator stuttered.

El-Amin shoved Tariq ahead of him, up the corridor steps. Each step was a monumental effort, their legs leaden, as if the tomb itself were trying to pull them back into its depths. The light of the surface cut through the dust like salvation. Behind them, the darkness of the tomb remained silent, but no one dared look back.

2

Tara paused, one gloved hand pressed against the stone, her flashlight beam cutting across the passage ahead. The air hung heavy with cold damp and the metallic tang of oxidized rock. Water dripped in the distance, steady and rhythmic. This far down, the mine should have been narrow, rough-hewn, jagged with the scars of pickaxe and blasting drill. It should have felt industrial, human, and relatively new.

But this tunnel was different.

Her husband Alex stepped up beside her, sweeping his own light across the walls. "This wall is way smoother than a typical mine."

"Yeah," Tara agreed. Her voice was quiet, absorbed by the oppressive silence.

The passage was old. It was the kind of age you didn't just see, but you could feel. Not in the temperature or the structure, but in the way the stone breathed. The ceiling dipped just enough to make them hunch slightly. The floor sloped unevenly, a loose scatter of ancient gravel beneath thick layers of dust. Their boots left crisp, lonely tracks behind them.

No one had walked this way in a very long time.

The IAA sent them to Iceland after some amateur explorers reported bizarre events, including time loss and unexplained visual and auditory hallucinations inside a sealed 19th-century mine. The initial report had been flagged as a probable hoax, but the details were too specific, too consistent across the group to be dismissed entirely.

The case that sealed it for IAA director Tommy Schultz was when one man emerged from the tunnels clutching a carved stone fragment he had no memory of retrieving. The markings on it matched no known Nordic system.

When Tara and Alex arrived on site, they initially attempted to conduct an interview with the man, but that produced nothing helpful, and the passage of time hadn't brought back any memories of his time in the mine. He spoke of the experience like a phantom limb, a void where a traumatic memory was supposed to be.

After a few more conversations, including with the explorers who experienced the hallucinations, the initial hypothesis was that there could be some kind of chemical, or perhaps a hallucinogenic gas escaping from deeper within the earth.

But after conducting tests of the area, those answers evaporated. There were no signs of chemicals or gas in or around the mines.

Alex moved ahead slowly, his voice low, eyes focused on the corridor and the darkness beyond the reach of his light. "This wasn't carved by miners," he said, studying the walls on either side.

Tara nodded, trailing her hand along the wall. "Agreed." She ran her gloved hand along the wall again. "Miners wouldn't waste time shaping walls this smooth. Not when they were blasting for ore. Every ounce of their effort would have been focused on extraction, not aesthetics."

Alex nodded. "And look at the ceiling. No chisel marks, no tool scoring, no soot from lanterns. Nothing about this says 19th-century industrial."

"The floor's wrong too," she added. "It's not graded. It doesn't pitch for drainage."

They both stepped back, scanning the corridor in silence. The beams of their flashlights danced across the unsettlingly perfect surfaces, revealing no flaws, no history of labor.

"This wasn't dug out to extract anything," Alex said. "It was carved for access."

Tara looked ahead into the gloom. "Or containment." The word sent a chill through both of them as they pushed forward.

The tunnel stretched another twenty meters before narrowing at a slight angle, then turning sharply left. The temperature had dropped noticeably since they entered the off-grid section, despite that temperatures underground usually stabilized down to around 100 feet. Their breath fogged in front of them now. The silence was deeper too. Not the stillness of quiet, but the quiet of forgotten things.

They turned a corner, and stopped. The corridor ended in a wall of cut stone, perfectly smooth and rectangular. It was not a cave wall, not a collapsed tunnel. It was a door.

Tara stepped closer, crouching to examine the seam. The slab had been placed with precision, fitted so tightly into the tunnel's end that not even a thread of light passed through its edges. Her flashlight revealed faint markings on the surface—weathered carvings; geometric and symmetrical.

Alex scanned the wall with his multispectral sensor. The screen flickered, then steadied.

"Not basalt. Not iron. This was brought in from somewhere else."

"But why? And who brought it here?"

"The old million-dollar question," he drawled.

Tara looked closer at the carvings. They appeared to be some kind of runes, but not those typical of Scandinavian origin. They possessed a different logic; a sharper, more mathematical quality.

"We need to be alert," she said. "This is where the others started having those hallucinations."

"What do you think this is?" Alex asked behind her.

She didn't answer right away.

Tara reached into her pack, pulled out a soft brush, and gently began clearing the dust from the symbols. One of them, near the base of the slab, looked almost like a human eye. Not stylized like Egyptian iconography. More primal. A staring shape enclosed by curved lines, as if pressed into the stone by force rather than carved with a tool. It felt less like art and more like a warning label.

"Help me get the other scanner on this," she said. "If this is a door, we need to know what's behind it."

Alex dropped his pack and knelt beside her, already assembling the portable GPR unit.

The wall waited, silent and cold, guarding something buried far older than the mine around it.

Alex adjusted the sensor plate on the scanner, and pressed it gently against the stone. The machine chirped twice, then began its sweep, sending low-frequency pulses through the slab. Tara watched the readout unfold in pale green lines across the handheld screen.

At first, there was nothing. Just the dense consistency of rock and compression. Then the pattern shifted.

Alex frowned. "Hold on."

The display showed a pocket, an open void roughly four meters beyond the slab, its dimensions squared, the edges too regular to be natural. It was a small room.

"Well," he said, "if there was any question as to whether or not this was manmade, I think we just cleared that up. That's obviously a chamber."

He pointed to a shape in the upper right corner of the scan. It wasn't clear, just a denser form against the empty space. Compact. Upright. Humanoid.

Tara narrowed her eyes. "That could be a statue."

"Or a burial."

They looked at each other in silence for a moment before Alex spoke up again. "But if it's a tomb, that doesn't account for what happened to those people before."

Tara stepped back and looked again at the slab. The fit, the seal, the imported material, it all suggested a different purpose than a typical tomb or forgotten shrine.

She spoke quietly. "Whatever this is, it's much older than the mine. I wonder if this was why they shut operations down so long ago."

Alex nodded slowly. "And tried to cover it up."

"Or were told to stay away."

She turned and swept her light across the tunnel again, now seeing it differently. The sudden shift in the tunnel's direction, the way the walls grew smoother, less fractured—this wasn't an accident. The miners had discovered something and rerouted to avoid it.

Alex packed the scanner while Tara continued documenting the symbols with her camera. The eye-shaped marking at the base of the slab now seemed more like a warning. Not stylized or sacred. More like a lock. A seal.

"You okay?" Alex asked, looking over at his wife.

"Yeah. I'm good. You?"

"Yeah. Just checking. How long was it those people were down here before they started flipping out?"

Tara thought for a second before answering. "I don't remember if they said or not. Just that weird things started happening."

Tara knelt again, this time focusing on the two elongated glyphs etched vertically into either side of the slab. They looked like mirrored runes at first glance—each with sharp angles and curling tails—but something about them bothered her.

She adjusted her headlamp and leaned in. "They're not symmetrical," she murmured.

Alex looked up from the gear case. "What isn't?"

"These glyphs. See how the left one is slightly higher?" She traced the air beside it with a gloved finger. "And the ends aren't quite matching."

He walked over, brushing the dust off his hands. "Could be a sloppy carver. Or maybe it shifted over time?"

Tara didn't answer right away. Her gaze remained fixed. Something was gnawing at her. Not just intellectually—but a feeling. A subtle pull in her gut.

She reached out again, fingers hovering just above the stone. A fine line caught her eye, barely perceptible in the gloom. There was a seam; a paper-thin shadow between the glyph and the rest of the slab. It was too clean to be a crack. It looked deliberate.

"This part isn't attached," she said softly.

Alex blinked. "You mean like an inlay?"

"No. I think it's mechanical."

She pressed gently against the right-side glyph. It didn't move.

Tara shifted her weight and pushed a little harder, expecting the same resistance—but it gave. Just a hair. A coarse, gritty sound followed, like rock grinding against dried mortar.

Alex tilted his head. "Was that—?"

Tara tried again, this time with both hands. The glyph budged. Not much, but enough. It sank inward, maybe half an inch, and she felt it catch, like a key waiting for the second turn. She stopped.

"You hear that?" she asked.

The tunnel had gone strangely still. Not silent—there were still occasional creaks in the rock, the distant drip of condensation—but there was a tension now. The kind of silence that feels like it's watching you.

Alex stepped beside her. "Try the other one."

Tara hesitated. Then she moved to the opposite glyph. Her gloved fingers brushed across its edge, searching for the same seam. There it was.

She applied pressure. This one moved more freely, as if recently disturbed. A thin layer of dust broke loose and scattered down the face of the stone.

Carefully, she pushed until the two glyphs aligned perfectly—tips aimed at one another, forming a kind of elongated eye with no pupil. She heard another click. Not mechanical. Deeper. Internal.

A breath of air hissed from behind the slab. They both turned to face it fully now. Nothing happened.

The slab didn't open. No doors slid away. But something had changed. The air was different, slightly cooler, and touched with the faintest trace of ozone, like the sky before a storm.

Tara took a step back.

"Did we just unlock something?" Alex asked.

Tara's voice was barely above a whisper. "I think so."

They waited. Five seconds. Ten. Still nothing.

Suddenly, they felt a vibration from within the ground. A sound so deep it wasn't heard so much as felt, resonating in their chest cavities and molars.

They looked at each other.

"Whatever that was," he said, "I don't think it was supposed to be touched."

Tara brushed the dust from the lower half of the eye-shaped glyph with the edge of her glove, then leaned in close. "There's a second one," she said. "Underneath the first."

Alex stepped beside her, angling his flashlight. "Same symbol?"

"No," she said slowly. "It's similar. Same eye shape, but fractured, like it's been split in half down the middle. One side is etched shallow, almost worn away. The other is deeper. Sharper."

He crouched beside her. "Like it was carved at two different times."

"And by two different hands."

She didn't say it aloud, but the resemblance to a mechanical seam, not just a symbol, nagged at her. Not decoration. Function.

Tara reached into her bag, pulling out a small bristle brush and a thin chisel. "Help me clear this."

They worked in silence, brushing sediment, sweeping away loose grit and time-packed debris. The deeper they went, the more the glyph revealed itself: a complete oval, bisected vertically by a narrow groove. On either side of the groove, strange linear strokes radiated like lashes, no known script. Not Nordic. Not Egyptian. Not cuneiform.

Alex sat back on his heels. "What do you think?"

Tara reached forward, tracing the central groove with her gloved fingertip. Then she pressed her thumb lightly on the left half of the eye. Nothing.

She tried the right half. Still nothing.

Alex leaned closer. "Wait. Shine the light again, but angle it lower."

She tilted her flashlight. Shadows lengthened, and then shimmered.

Thin veins in the stone, imperceptible before, began to glow faintly under the angled beam. Phosphorescent mineral threads, like tiny capillaries, traced out from the central eye-glyph and pulsed softly in greenish blue. The glow arced up the slab, disappearing into its edges.

"Did we... trigger that?" Alex whispered.

Tara shook her head. "I don't think it's from the light."

She pressed the pad of her thumb firmly into the center groove where both halves of the glyph met. For a second, nothing. Then—

Click.

The sound was so faint it barely registered. But they both heard it. And then the slab shifted.

It didn't swing or crack. It simply began to lower, sinking into the floor like it was being pulled by something deep below. Dust whispered down the walls as the massive stone receded silently, leaving behind a widening dark void.

They stood frozen, flashlights sweeping the emerging chamber.

"I think that unlocked it" Alex said, voice tight.

Tara stared ahead. "Me too."

As the slab sank flush with the stone floor, the phosphorescent veins pulsed once more, then dimmed, fading into the rock as though they had never been there. The silence that followed was impossibly still, as if even the air was holding its breath.

Beyond the opening, the tunnel widened into a rough-hewn antechamber. The walls were blackened stone, but smooth, not blasted by dynamite or cracked by age. At the far end, another archway loomed.

Tara flicked off her light for a second. The inside of the chamber was pitch-black. No natural glow. No airflow. Absolute silence.

She clicked it back on. "Let's go."

Alex hesitated for half a second, then followed her through.

Crossing the threshold felt like stepping through a veil. The air shifted—colder, denser. The smell changed, too. No longer the musty damp of old earth, but something metallic; sharp, almost electric.

Behind them, the slab remained lowered. They moved in silence, sweeping their lights across the chamber's interior.

And then they saw it. Near the center of the room stood an enormous stone sarcophagus; taller than Tara and wider than a man's outstretched arms. And surrounding it, etched into the walls, floor, and even the coffin itself, were more glyphs.

Some were unmistakably Egyptian. But others... others defied origin.

Tara's breath caught in her throat. Alex turned toward her, but said nothing.

Tara moved slowly around the sarcophagus, camera raised, the beam from her flashlight catching every carved groove and jagged line. She wasn't sure what disturbed her more, the age of the thing, or the eerie sense of precision behind its construction. The stone wasn't cracked or weathered. This wasn't a burial made centuries ago and left to rot. This was deliberate, preserved.

Alex ran his hand along the wall beside the opening, eyes scanning the glyphs etched there. "Okay," he said, squinting, "we've got definite Egyptian here. Early Dynastic, maybe even Naqada period."

She nodded, still circling. "That fits. The lotus bloom here, the falcon motif there. But look at the spacing."

He stepped back to get a wider view. "It's wrong."

"Exactly," she said. "It's as if someone copied the style without understanding the structure. Like they were imitating something they saw... or trying to blend it with something else."

Alex turned back toward the sarcophagus, jaw tightening. "Why is that symbol on the lid?"

Tara stepped up beside him.

Near the center of the stone coffin, etched deeper than the others, was a circular pattern with an eye again. But not the protective Eye of Horus. This one was stretched vertically and surrounded by jagged spines. Around it, the same split-glyph pattern they had seen at the slab. Almost like a mirrored keyhole. Or a warning seal.

Tara reached out and hovered her hand just above the surface. The air above the symbol felt colder than the rest of the room.

She didn't touch it.

Alex moved to the side of the coffin, brushing dust from a cluster of unfamiliar markings. "These... aren't Egyptian," he said. "Not Nordic either. In fact, no script I know of."

Tara stepped over. "It's not script. Look—each one has repeated spacing. Identical patterns."

"Coordinates?" he asked.

She frowned. "Maybe. Or a sequence."

Alex lowered his voice. "You think this is a tomb?"

Tara looked back at the shape of the sarcophagus. The lid was seamless. No indication of how it had been opened—or even if it could be. The entire thing looked carved from a single block.

"I don't know," she admitted. "I don't know what this is."

Alex tilted his head. "That doesn't look like stone."

He pointed to the corner edge where the lid met the body. Tara leaned closer. At first glance it appeared gray like the rest, but under her flashlight, it shimmered faintly—metallic, almost like hematite or some strange iron alloy.

"That's not granite," she said quietly.

"No chisel marks either."

"And no inscriptions about who's buried here. No names. No offerings. No funerary text."

Alex glanced toward the exit. "What if it's not a tomb?" he asked. "What if it's a prison?"

They both went still. The word echoed inside her skull like it had been waiting to be said aloud.

"A prison?" she asked. "For who?"

"Or what?" he added.

Whoever or whatever was inside the sarcophagus wasn't honored —by usual funerary ordinances—instead, it looked as if it was designed to contain something, or someone.

Alex turned slowly, surveying the walls again. "These aren't prayers. These are warnings."

Tara stepped back, breath catching in her throat. A dozen thoughts flooded her mind about the auditory hallucinations, the time loss, the panic reports from earlier expeditions. The fragments of the story that had seemed like paranoid delusion on the surface now clicked into place with horrifying clarity.

"What if it's not psychological?" she said, eyes wide. "What's in this thing that could have caused all those symptoms?"

She raised her camera and snapped more photos, capturing every inch of the lid, the glyphs, the walls. The tension in her chest wouldn't ease. It felt like the chamber was pushing inward, like gravity had doubled. And it was pulling them toward the sarcophagus.

"Do you feel that?" she asked. "How it seems we're being pulled closer to it?"

"Yeah," Alex said. "And I don't like it. Maybe we should go, come back later with some more equipment. Maybe some hazmat suits. We have no idea what we're dealing with here."

She didn't answer. Instead, Tara moved closer to the sarcophagus. She stared at it with vapid eyes, as if entranced by something. Alex found himself moving closer to the ancient container as well.

He managed to stop himself short of the sarcophagus, and looked down at his watch.

"Uh, Tara?"

She looked over at him, her eyes still vacant. "What?"

"Look at your watch."

The emptiness in her expression shifted to one of confusion. Then she looked down at her watch, and gasped.

The digital screen was glitching, flashing random times and dates. But what was more unsettling was between the flashes, there was the outline of a face, as if shrouded in shadow and mist. It was a face of impossible age and profound malevolence, and for a fraction of a second, Tara felt as if it were looking not at her, but out of her own eyes.

3

I don't think we should stay here," Alex said. His voice was strained, cutting through the heavy silence that had fallen since their discovery of the face on the watch.

"We can't leave now," Tara countered. Her gaze was still locked on the sarcophagus, a mix of academic fascination and a deeper, more unsettling pull she didn't want to name. "We need to find out what's inside this?"

"Look, I get it. That's our job. But something is very wrong here. It's like this place is messing with time itself. And I don't know what the heck that face is, but it's giving me the creeps."

She shook off her fear, a conscious act of will against the tide of instinct screaming at her to run, and resumed her study of the sarcophagus, searching for a way to open it. She hesitated, just for a second. Then she shook off the chill crawling up her spine and stepped closer to the coffin, running her gloved fingers along the edge. The metallic-like surface still felt cold, but it no longer vibrated under her hand. That didn't make her feel any better.

"There has to be a way to open it," she said.

Tara crouched low beside the sarcophagus, trailing her fingers along the side as she studied the glyphs carved with surgical precision into the dark stone. They weren't decorative or ceremonial. These were tight, controlled, mathematical, like someone had coded equations in stone.

She tilted her head and began to whisper, instinctively sounding out the symbols. The syllables felt alien on her tongue, yet strangely familiar, as if she were recalling a language she had never learned.

"Sekem-na... tef khepra... idun-serekh..."

The moment the last syllable left her lips, the stone beneath her hand warmed slightly. Not hot, just a degree above body temperature, enough to feel unnatural.

Alex stiffened. "What did you just say?"

"I... don't know," she whispered. The words had come from her, but she felt as though she had merely been a vessel for them.

A sound rose from the sarcophagus. It was deep and mechanical, like pressure equalizing far below the earth. The heavy lid shifted with unnatural ease, sliding to one side as if moved by a mechanism beneath the floor.

No gas. No burst of ancient air. Just silence and motion.

Inside, nestled in a carved depression that fit it exactly, lay a smooth black stone the size of a grapefruit. Polished to a mirror sheen, it seemed to absorb the beam from Tara's flashlight rather than reflect it. It was a perfect void, a sphere of absolute nothingness that seemed to drink the light around it.

"Is that obsidian?" Alex asked.

She shook her head. "No. Obsidian fractures. This is... perfect. Like it was poured."

Alex moved closer, then stopped short. He didn't want to look at it directly. Not fear, something deeper. A primal warning, like standing too close to the edge of a high ledge. His hindbrain was screaming at him that this object was fundamentally wrong, a violation of natural law.

Tara, however, was transfixed. She reached forward but didn't touch it. Just hovered her hand above the stone.

A subtle vibration met her palm, not physical, but sensory, like the moment before a static shock or the hum of sub-bass through your chest. Then she noticed the lid.

Turning her light upward, she saw the underside was lined with carvings. Not clean like the exterior glyphs, but frantic, etched in different hands, some shallow and erratic, others deep and deliberate.

"Some of these were carved from the inside," she whispered.

Alex's voice came low behind her. "That's not a burial."

She looked at him. "It's a container."

Tara nodded slowly, her pulse quickening.

Then the stone pulsed, just once, a silent breath escaping from deep within it.

"Any ideas why it's doing that?" Alex asked, his voice shaking.

Tara didn't answer. She remained crouched beside the sarcophagus, unmoving. Her eyes were locked on the object, her breath slow and steady, like she was syncing with it.

Alex glanced at her, then back to the stone. "You feel that, right?"

She nodded, slowly. "It's like... pressure. But not physical. Like a thought trying to force its way into your head."

He swallowed. "Okay, now you're creeping me out."

She stood, brushing the dust from her pants. "Whatever this is, it's not a relic. It's a mechanism. Maybe biological. Maybe technological. Maybe both. And it wants something."

Alex narrowed his eyes. "Wants?"

"It's calling to us," Tara said. "I've felt that before, with certain megalithic structures. But this is stronger. Like it knows us."

Alex shook his head, backing up another step. "You're talking like it's sentient."

She looked over at him. "What if it is?"

"I'm losing signal on my tablet," Tara said, looking down at the glitching screen. She tried toggling through the menus, but the device was frozen on a flashing screen of jumbled characters. Not random. Structured. Familiar.

Glyphs. The same ones etched inside the lid.

"Tara," Alex said, his voice quieter now. "What if this is a threshold?"

She looked up.

"A doorway," he continued. "Not literally. But something... quantum. Nonlinear. Look at everything we've seen, glitching electronics, distorted time signatures, your watch flashing that face."

"I know," she said. Her voice had changed. Less scientific now. More reverent.

"It's like it's... waiting."

They stood together in silence. The tomb was still. The air had grown warm. Too warm. Like they were standing beneath a desert sun instead of a mountain.

Tara's hand drifted toward the stone, trembling.

"I think we have to see," she whispered.

Alex stared at her.

"Together," she added. "Same time."

He hesitated, then gave a slow, reluctant nod.

And without another word, they reached out, and touched the stone.

The moment their fingers met the stone, the chamber vanished.

There was no flash of light, no tremor in the earth, just a sudden and complete rupture from the world they knew.

Tara gasped, except there was no air, no sound. Only motion.

They stood on a floating platform of what looked like obsidian glass, suspended in a churning void. Above them, stars exploded into galaxies and collapsed back into nothing. Below, rivers of liquid fire twisted into chains that wrapped around shifting silhouettes, human and not. Time did not pass here. It folded. A Viking longship sailed on a sea of sand. A pyramid made of chrome reflected a sky of burning comets.

Fractals of color, geometry, and impossible architecture surrounded them in a dome that felt both infinite and suffocating. Cities bloomed and decayed in the blink of an eye. A Roman legion marched through a forest that turned into a neon-lit metropolis. A pharaoh crowned himself king on a throne made of glass. A boy pulled a blade from a stone, and then the blade turned into a serpent and swallowed the world.

Tara turned toward Alex. Her mouth moved, her words arrived seconds later, disjointed and fragmented.

"Where... are we?"

"I... don't know."

His voice felt like it echoed not just through space, but through selves. Versions of himself appeared in flickers beside him, young, old, broken, victorious. Tara, too, splintered and duplicated. One wore a military uniform. Another floated in what looked like a stasis chamber, bald and wired into machines.

But their real selves remained linked, anchored to the black stone and somehow still present in their original bodies. They could feel it. A tether. A thin, fragile connection back to the cold, dark reality of the tomb.

The sky above them peeled open. They both looked up. A massive eye stared back at them.

It wasn't human. Not even close. It was layered, like a geode cracked open, revealing iris upon iris, depth beyond depth. It blinked once, slowly and deliberately, and the world shifted again.

Now they stood in a scorched field where machines harvested bones. Men in strange robes chanted around a pillar of smoke. Then, in an instant, they were submerged in an ocean of static and whispers, the weight of forgotten civilizations pressing in on all sides.

Tara reached out toward one of the flickering visions. It showed a lush green valley where people wore clothing made from woven gold. Her fingers passed through it like mist, but her eyes widened.

"I know this place," she whispered. "I've seen this place in a dream."

Alex's pulse thundered in his ears. His knees buckled. He couldn't breathe. Couldn't process.

"What is this?"

"The Well of Time," a voice said.

Neither of them had spoken it. The voice echoed inside them. Ancient, vast, and utterly indifferent.

Tara stumbled back, still touching the stone, her eyes rolling white for a moment. Her body spasmed. "Alex!"

He tried to reach for her, but the ground beneath them cracked like glass, fracturing into puzzle pieces that spun outward into the dark. More visions.

An island surrounded by fire. A spacecraft lifting from a ziggurat. A jungle village where a stone monolith hovered just above the canopy, humming like a tuning fork. All timelines. All possible. All real. The tether thinned.

Alex felt his mind pulling apart, like his consciousness was being sliced into ribbons and scattered across realities.

He focused on Tara. She was still locked in place, her hand pressed to the stone, eyes wide, lips trembling as if reciting something silently. He shouted, but his voice was pulled sideways. He tried again, this time shoving all his energy into a single thought.

Tara.

She looked at him.

And in that moment, clarity. He had to break free.

Alex turned his focus inward. Grounded himself in sensation. The pressure of his palm against the smooth surface. The pounding of his heart. The scent of ancient dust still lingering in his sinuses.

He gritted his teeth. And tore his hand away. The chamber returned in a single violent snap.

Alex screamed as he fell backward, slamming onto the stone floor of the Icelandic tomb. His chest heaved. Sweat poured down his face. His limbs twitched involuntarily as if they were still vibrating from some unseen current. The sensory whiplash was agonizing, the sudden return of gravity and solid reality a brutal shock to his system.

The room was spinning. But it was real again. Solid. He turned to look.

Tara was still touching the stone. Still trapped. Her face was a mask of placid awe, a faint, pulsing light reflecting in her wide, unseeing eyes.

And her lips were moving, chanting something in a language he didn't recognize.

Alex moved fast, hurrying to her side.

"Tara?" he said, but she didn't respond.

Her body began to shake.

Not just tremble, but convulse. Like something deep within her was vibrating against the laws of physics. Her eyes fluttered, unfocused and glassy. Her fingertips twitched against the stone. A low hum filled the chamber, so low it wasn't audible so much as felt, through bone, through marrow.

Fear pumped through his veins. He didn't know what would happen if he tried to pull her away from the stone, but he didn't have a choice.

Alex reached down, grabbed her wrists, and tugged. For a second, nothing happened. Then the world exploded.

A thunderclap of invisible force knocked them backward. Not outward, downward. As if the chamber itself had punched them into the stone floor. Dust lifted from every crack and crevice, curling into the air like rising smoke.

They hit hard, landing in a tangle of limbs and gasps.

Tara let out a sharp cry, instinctively curling into a defensive posture. Alex rolled to his side, coughing, blinking through the haze of stone dust and whatever else had been thrown into the air by the strange blast.

"Tara?" he wheezed again, voice raspy.

She coughed, then opened her eyes. Still distant. Still wide with that awful mixture of awe and fear. But she was back.

He reached for her hand, and she squeezed it. Hard.

"You okay?" he asked.

She nodded, then shook her head. "I don't know. I..." Her voice caught. She sat up slowly, breathing hard, her chest heaving.

"It was like... a billion moments stacked together," she whispered. "Like I was standing at the center of a vortex of time."

Alex rubbed the back of his neck. "I saw things too. Cities, people, events. Timelines stacked like playing cards. Some of them... impossible. Some of them felt like memories, but they weren't mine."

He looked toward the stone, now sitting quiet inside the sarcophagus, as if it had never moved, never pulsed, never drawn them in. But it had. And something had changed. The glyphs on the inside of the lid were glowing.

Not bright, not warm, but unmistakably alive. Like veins lit from within.

Tara stared at them. "They're active now. We triggered it."

They both sat in silence for a moment, collecting themselves, letting the oppressive stillness of the chamber settle again.

Alex finally broke the silence.

"We need to get out of here."

Tara didn't answer right away, then nodded.

They both stood, brushing themselves off. Tara reached for her tablet again; it flickered but powered back on. Still sluggish. Still glitching. But alive.

They turned back once more toward the sarcophagus. The stone sat silently, matte black and unmoving. The air no longer pulsed. But the glyphs... they were still glowing.

Tara took a slow breath. "This isn't Egyptian. It's not Sumerian. It's not anything I've ever seen before."

"It's pre-everything," Alex said. "Maybe even pre-human."

They stared at the artifact a moment longer. Then, from deep within the chamber, something shifted. Not the artifact. Not the room. The mountain.

A faint rumble vibrated up through their boots, slow and deep, like a groan in the bones of the earth itself. It passed in seconds, but it left them both frozen.

Tara took a step back from the sarcophagus, still breathing hard, her fingers trembling at her sides.

Alex moved beside her. "We need to get out of here. Now."

She didn't argue.

They turned and began retracing their steps toward the corridor. The air felt different, thicker, like a thousand-year storm was building underground. It wasn't just the staleness of a sealed tomb anymore. It was pressure. A weight bearing down from all sides, as if the stone walls had drawn breath and now held it, waiting to exhale.

Their boots scraped across the floor as they moved quickly past the glowing glyphs, now pulsating with faint rhythmic light.

Alex glanced at them. "Still glowing."

"I know," Tara said, not slowing. "And they weren't before. We activated something."

They entered the tunnel they'd carved earlier that week, one that cut through the collapsed section of the mine leading to the chamber. Alex ducked under a wooden support beam, nearly tripping over the mess of gear they'd left earlier. A helmet rolled across the floor behind him without being touched.

Tara didn't look back.

The walls here were closer, narrower. They'd reinforced them with temporary struts when they first accessed the site, but now those supports groaned. Metal on stone. Stone on stone. A single light bulb strung along a temporary cable began to flicker above them.

"Move," Alex said.

They broke into a run.

Behind them, a low sound emerged. It wasn't mechanical, not seismic, it seemed organic. It was like a whisper from beneath the rock, a resonance that bypassed the ears and went straight into the skull. It carried no language. Just feeling.

Dread.

They pushed harder.

At the end of the tunnel, they burst into the operations room—a makeshift camp set up inside the main shaft of the old Icelandic mine. A desk scattered with notebooks. A table with excavation tools, two cold cups of coffee, and a battered satellite phone sitting atop a cracked pelican case.

Alex dove for it. Tara slumped against the table, heart pounding in her ears.

Alex was already dialing. The signal light blinked red, searching. Then, green. It rang once. Twice.

"Come on," Alex muttered.

Click.

"Tommy Schultz," came the voice on the other end; calm, Southern, and familiar.

"Tommy, it's Alex," he said. "Tara's with me. We're in Iceland. We found something."

"You're early," Tommy replied. "You weren't supposed to check in for another day."

"We weren't planning to," Alex said. "But something's wrong. We opened a chamber. Not part of the mine. Something older. And we found a sarcophagus, but it's not a coffin. It's something else."

There was a pause on the line.

"How bad?" Tommy asked.

Alex glanced at Tara. She nodded.

"It's worse than bad," he said. "Whatever this thing is, it activated. Tara and I touched the object inside and it showed us... I don't even know how to explain it. Timelines. Places. Events. Simultaneous realities. We were inside them."

"It felt like our minds were getting peeled apart," Tara said, stepping beside Alex so she could be heard on the line. "This is not a simple tomb. And this wasn't made by nineteenth-century miners. This thing might predate the Ice Age. Maybe even humanity."

Tommy exhaled slowly. "You saying it's dangerous?"

"It nearly killed us," Alex said. "And we think it triggered something seismic. We felt it. The whole place vibrated like it was waking up."

Another pause. Then: "I'll send a containment team. May need to have Sean on site for that one."

"Understood," Alex said.

"So, are you two really okay?"

They glanced at each other for a second, then both nodded. "Yeah. We're good. Just another in a growing list of mind-bending experiences."

"Well, I didn't want to spring this on you, but once we get the containment team on site, I have another project to look into if you're up for it."

"So soon?" Tara asked.

"I know it's unusual," Tommy said, "but I got a call from Egypt. There's something strange going on, and an old acquaintance of mine needs your expertise."

"Egypt?" Alex asked.

"It'll be warmer than where you are now," Tommy joked.

"No kidding."

The two glanced at each other again, then shrugged.

"Sure," Tara said. "Why not?" It felt less like a choice and more like the only way to outrun the memory of what they had just experienced.

"Great. I'll send you all the details. You can have a look en route. I know this isn't a smooth transition. Usually you take some down time after something like this."

"We're good," she said. "Don't worry about us."

"I try not to."

4

The desert heat crawled across the landscape, leaving wavy mirages flickering above the ground in the distance. It was a stark and brutal contrast to the frigid Icelandic mine they had left less than forty-eight hours ago, a shift in climate so abrupt it felt like stepping onto another world.

Tara stepped out of the truck and let the warm breeze slide over her skin. The air was dry, metallic, and laced with grit that scratched at her throat the moment she inhaled. Pale sunlight spilled across the low plateau ahead, casting long shadows from battered tents and equipment crates that looked more abandoned than active.

Nothing in the scene buzzed with life. No voices. No radio chatter. No clinking of tools. Just the wind whispering past the canvas like it remembered something no one had asked it to recall. It was the silence of a place holding its breath.

Alex Simms slammed the passenger door and walked around to her side. He scanned the horizon, adjusting his sunglasses, then looked over the small encampment that sat just west of the crumbling ridge.

"This feels... cheerful," he muttered.

Tara didn't respond. Her eyes were locked on the man standing alone near the cluster of tents, just beyond the perimeter line. Arms crossed. Shoulders drawn in against the wind.

"Is that him?" Alex asked.

"I believe so."

Dr. Hatem El-Amin ambled toward them with a welcoming but cautious grin on his face.

He wasn't what she expected. Not exactly. She knew the name, of course, a respected field archaeologist with a reputation for quiet rigor and a deep respect for Egyptian antiquity. She'd seen a few lectures, read a paper or two, but standing here, he looked less like the head of a world-class dig and more like a man who hadn't slept in days. His eyes, usually sharp and analytical in the photos she'd seen, were shadowed with a deep weariness that had nothing to do with lack of sleep and everything to do with what he had witnessed.

He was tall and lean, built like someone who'd spent more years in the sun than under any roof. His linen jacket was stained at the elbows, and his scarf had been pulled loose to let the heat escape. His face, lined by sun and experience, was calm, but there was something behind the eyes. Something he was keeping tucked away.

Dr. Hatem El-Amin stood with the posture of a man used to leading digs in hostile climates. Lean and sun-darkened, with deep-set eyes and a voice that rarely rose above measured calm, he carried the quiet authority of someone who'd seen too many things buried that should have stayed that way.

"Alex. Tara." His voice was calm but weary. "Thank you both so much for coming so quickly. I hope it wasn't too much trouble?"

"No trouble at all, sir," Tara answered.

"We had just finished a case in Iceland when Tommy called and told us about your... situation here."

"Yes," the doctor said, twisting his head one way then the other, as if scanning the land around them for trouble.

"Are you hungry? Need something to drink?"

"Some food would be nice," Tara said.

"Excellent. We'll get you fixed up right away. It's nothing fancy out here, I'm afraid, but it fills the belly."

He motioned for them to follow him, then turned and began walking toward the largest tent in the middle of the encampment.

They moved through the camp in silence, the wind flapping at the tent edges and kicking up little ghosts of dust along the worn footpaths. A few workers lingered near a table stacked with buckets and tools, but none of them spoke. They just watched, their gazes heavy with a mixture of fear and resentment, as if Tara and Alex were fresh lambs being led to a slaughter they themselves had only narrowly escaped.

Alex couldn't be sure, but he felt like Dr. El-Amin was avoiding looking down into the pit where the dig had been ongoing for the last few months.

Tara noticed too, but she found herself staring down into it as they passed. The main shaft entrance sat just fifty yards to the east, reinforced with scaffolding and shadowed under a canvas sunshade. No one went near it. No one even glanced in its direction. It might as well have been a bomb crater.

Alex looked like he was about to say something, then thought better of it.

They reached the main tent, not the largest, but clearly the one El-Amin was living out of. The flap was rolled and pinned open. Inside, the temperature dropped slightly, and the air grew heavier with the scent of sand, sweat, and canvas. There was a small desk, a cot, a fold-out chair, and a rack of maps leaned against the center pole. One of the maps was torn at the corner, folded too many times, the edges marked in thick red ink.

El-Amin stepped to the side and motioned them in. He still hadn't spoken. Tara entered first, Alex just behind her.

El-Amin walked to the desk. After offering Alex and Tara some food and water, he picked up a steel mug, and poured water from a sun-warmed canteen. He drank slowly, wiped his mouth, and set the mug down with careful precision. Only then did he speak.

"I want to be clear about something before we begin," he said, voice low. "I didn't call you here because I'm frightened. I've worked in Saqqara for a while now. I know the myths. The curses. The rumors. I've walked through tombs that hadn't been touched in four thousand years."

Tara waited.

El-Amin looked at her. Then at Alex.

"I called you because I'm not sure what I heard down there... was human."

No one moved. Alex slowly lowered his pack to the ground.

El-Amin took another sip from his mug, then set it aside again and leaned against the edge of the desk. "The assistant. Tariq. He's still here. Alive. Breathing. But not the same."

"What does that mean?" Tara asked.

"You'll see for yourself soon enough. But first, I want to tell you exactly what happened, from the moment we uncovered the chamber to the moment I sealed it again."

Alex raised an eyebrow. "You sealed it back up?"

"I had to. No one else would go near it. And I didn't want anyone getting the idea to sneak down there. It's only a temporary barricade, mostly plastic. So, if someone really wanted to, they could do it."

Tara leaned forward, elbows on her knees. "Well, I guess that's us then."

El-Amin nodded. "I figured we should wait for the professionals in this sort of thing."

He stepped around to the back of the desk and opened a small field case. Inside were four neatly labeled notebooks and a hard drive wrapped in cloth. He placed them on the table one by one.

"This isn't just another tomb," he said. "It doesn't follow dynastic layouts. There are no inscriptions. No cartouches. No reliefs. And the material used to seal the chamber... it isn't limestone. It's lead. Thick and seamless."

Alex frowned. "Sealed with lead?"

"Yes. And the moment we opened it, something started whispering."

He let that hang in the air. Tara didn't speak.

El-Amin stared at the tent wall, eyes unfocused for just a moment. Then he said, "I need you to understand. This wasn't a noise.

It wasn't airflow. It wasn't trapped gas or seismic vibration. It said my name." He said it so quietly Tara almost didn't hear it, but the words carried the weight of an unshakable, terrifying truth.

Tara straightened.

"El-Amin," he said quietly. "From inside the sarcophagus." He looked down at the floor. "That's when Tariq collapsed."

Alex crossed his arms. "You didn't try to open it again?"

"No. Fight or flight kicked in. We chose flight."

The tent went quiet again. Outside, the wind picked up.

Tara exhaled slowly. "What happened next?"

"I dragged him out," El-Amin said. "I called in the site team. Told them it was a structural issue and ordered the shaft closed. Then I called the IAA."

Alex rubbed his face.

Tara stood. Her voice was quieter now. "You're absolutely sure what you heard... came from inside the sarcophagus?"

El-Amin didn't answer right away. His gaze remained on the floor, as if the answer were written there in the patterns of dust. The silence stretched until the canvas walls themselves seemed to lean in. Finally, he lifted his head.

"I know what I heard," he said. "And I know when Tariq opened his eyes again, they weren't his."

Tara's skin tightened at the phrasing. She tried to press him. "What do you mean?"

"You'll understand when you see him," El-Amin replied. His voice was calm, but it carried the weight of something he hadn't yet decided to believe. "Come."

He gathered the notebooks back into the case with practiced care, set the mug aside, and moved toward the tent flap. Tara and Alex followed without another word.

The camp outside was still devoid of activity. The same wind hissed through the guy ropes. The same workers leaned against crates or sat with their backs to the sun, each one pretending not to look at them but stealing glances all the same. Their faces bore the unease of people who had witnessed something they couldn't name and wished they hadn't.

As El-Amin walked, the workers gave him a wide berth. No one spoke. No one even gestured. It wasn't respect. It was distance.

"Where is he?" Tara asked, keeping her voice low.

El-Amin nodded toward a smaller tent set apart from the others, its flap tied shut against the breeze. Two lanterns stood on poles at either side, though in full daylight they looked absurd.

Tara felt Alex shift beside her. His jaw tightened. He had the look of a man bracing himself.

When they reached the tent, El-Amin hesitated at the entrance. He touched the canvas, fingers brushing the rough weave as if steadying himself. Then he turned.

"He hasn't said much since the incident," he said. "When he does, it isn't in Arabic. It isn't in any language I know."

Tara's stomach turned cold. "But you understand him?"

El-Amin shook his head, and a somber expression stretched across his face.

He untied the flap. The interior was dim, the air stale with sweat and kerosene. A cot sat against the far wall, a basin beside it half filled with water gone cloudy. The lantern light cast a trembling circle across the canvas, and in its glow, Tariq sat hunched, his back curved like a question mark.

He lifted his head at the sound of their entrance.

Tara froze.

His eyes had once been brown; she remembered seeing them in the personnel file. Now they were dulled, the irises pale as stone. His skin looked drained, stretched too tight across his cheekbones. He stared at her, and though he was breathing, though his chest rose and fell, the look in his eyes was not human recognition. It was reception, as if something behind them was waiting.

"Tariq," El-Amin said carefully.

The young man blinked. His lips parted. For a moment, no sound came. Then a whisper trickled out, a sound dry as the desert itself.

"El-Amin."

The name crawled from his throat, not spoken but pulled, as though someone else were using his mouth.

Alex shifted a step forward.

Tariq's head turned sharply toward him. His pale eyes fixed on Alex, and his lips moved again.

"Alex."

The whisper wasn't loud, but it filled the space, reverberating in Tara's chest like a pressure drop before a storm. Her training screamed at her to assess the threat, but her mind was reeling. How could he know their names? They had just arrived. No one had briefed him. Alex swore under his breath and took a half step back.

Tara's pulse hammered. She tried to hold the young man's gaze, tried to measure whether he was even aware of what he was saying. "Tariq," she said, voice steady. "Do you know where you are?"

The lips twitched. His gaze shifted past her—to nothing. Then, in a voice not his own, he said, "It waits."

The tent seemed to shrink around them.

Tara turned to El-Amin. His face was grim, unchanged. "You see why I called you," he said.

Outside, the wind surged, rattling the poles.

Tara took a breath, forcing control back into her voice. "We need to see the chamber."

El-Amin hesitated. His eyes moved back to Tariq, who still sat rigid on the cot, lips moving in soundless fragments. Finally, he gave a single nod.

"I know that's why I called you here, but you must be careful. I don't want this happening to you too. Whatever is down there isn't something to trifle with."

"Understood," Alex said. "We'll be careful."

With a sigh, El-Amin pulled the flap open and the sunlight stabbed in. Tara and Alex followed him out, the heat washing over them like a wall. The workers stared openly now, their silence heavier than before.

El-Amin set a steady course toward the scaffolding.

The shaft waited ahead, its mouth shadowed by the sagging canvas awning, dark and silent like the open throat of the earth.

None of the workers followed. Not one.

Tara felt Alex fall into step beside her. His voice was low, tight. "Do you ever think maybe we should try to find normal jobs? You know, ones that don't involve supernatural occurrences that could end up driving us to an asylum, or worse?"

She passed a quick smile, then returned her focus to the pit. "Sounds boring."

"Yeah, I know," he said, running a hand through his hair.

The sun slipped behind a cloud, dimming the plateau. For the first time since they'd arrived, the air felt cooler. Almost as if something beneath the ground had exhaled.

El-Amin stood by the scaffolding. For the first time since they'd met him, his composure cracked. He turned to face them, arms crossed tight, and shoulders rigid.

"I won't go back in there," he said flatly. "Not again."

Tara studied him. "You know the layout better than anyone."

His jaw tightened. "And I sealed it for a reason. Whatever is down there, whatever spoke, it's not of this world. I'm not trained to handle things like that. You'll have to go without me, but it isn't complicated. You'll find your way easily enough."

The wind gusted, carrying grit across their boots. Alex adjusted the strap on his pack, then looked to Tara. "So it's just us."

Tara's eyes stayed on El-Amin a moment longer, reading the strain behind his calm. He wasn't bluffing. He was finished.

She exhaled and turned to Alex. "Better be extra cautious with this one."

Alex nodded slowly. "Right. Would be good to tether ourselves to something or someone above ground."

"Good call," Tara said. She glanced back toward the tent where Tariq sat. Her chest tightened. "No one else here is willing to help?"

El-Amin shook his head once. "They won't go near it. Not after what happened. You'll be on your own. But, if you're going to use a rope or some kind of tether, perhaps I can get one of the men to help as long as I tell them we're going to stay well clear of the entrance."

Alex gave a humorless laugh. "Perfect. See what you can do, professor." He dug into his pack, pulling out a coil of climbing rope.

"Tommy rubbing off on you?" Tara asked.

Alex chuckled. "Hey, you never know when you might need a good rope."

"That's exactly what he would say." Her tone was wry. "We should use noise cancelling headphones," she added. "May or may not make a difference, but it's worth a shot."

Alex raised an eyebrow. "Headphones?"

She met his look. "If the whispers are real, if they're... targeted, we can't risk listening to them. Noise-cancelling will dampen most of it. It's better than nothing."

Alex turned the idea over, then shrugged. "Could block out warning sounds too. Falling rocks. Shifting supports."

"Which do you fear more—stone, or a voice that knows your name?" Tara asked.

"Fair point."

El-Amin finally spoke again, quieter now. "If you go, go soon. Before the light changes. The deeper you are when the sun falls, the worse it might get. I know I wouldn't want to be down there after dark."

Tara checked her watch. The hands ticked toward mid-afternoon. "Half an hour," she said.

Alex frowned. "You sure you don't want to wait until morning? Better rested, better light—"

"No," she said, cutting him off. "Let's do it now."

"You're the boss," he joked.

Then Alex frowned. He stared out into the distance to the east.

Tara noticed his expression, and followed his concerned gaze.

A dust cloud rose from the desert, churning up into the sky like a storm. At the base of it, six black SUVs roared toward the encampment. They moved in a tight, disciplined formation that spoke of military training, kicking up plumes of dust that looked like warning flares against the deepening sky.

"Who is that?" Tara wondered out loud.

El-Amin watched the approaching vehicles. "I don't know, but they look like they could be from the government. And they look like they're in a hurry."

"Are you expecting a visit from government representatives today?" Alex asked.

El-Amin tore his stare away from the oncoming storm, and met Alex's gaze. "No."

5

The vehicles rolled into the camp one after another, black frames shimmering beneath the desert sun. Their tires ground deep tracks into the sand, sending curls of dust drifting over the plateau. When the engines cut, silence spread even wider than before. It was a heavy, expectant silence, thick with unspoken questions.

No one spoke. No one asked who they were.

The passenger door of the lead SUV opened first. A man stepped out.

He moved with unhurried grace, slim and poised, the kind of presence that carried its own weight without needing to announce it. His shirt, white linen, sleeves rolled neatly at the elbows, caught the light. It was an impossible, deliberate cleanliness that spoke of immense power, a man who didn't simply travel through the desert but made the desert accommodate him. A scarf hung loose at his neck, the fabric shifting slightly with the breeze. His black hair was combed straight back, silver streaks at the temples catching pale fire in the sun. No hat, no dust clinging to him, as though the desert itself had been instructed not to touch him.

He removed his sunglasses with a small motion, folding them in one hand. His eyes swept the camp, slow and deliberate, until they found El-Amin, Tara, and Alex. He smiled faintly, as though reassured by what he saw.

Two men climbed out behind him, dressed in plain tactical gear, compact rifles slung low. Another pair emerged from the second vehicle. Their steps were practiced, their silence heavier than weapons alone.

The man in white approached, hands loosely clasped behind his back. When he stopped, the distance between him and the three archaeologists felt intentional, close enough to dominate, far enough to remain untouchable.

"Dr. El-Amin," he said smoothly, his Arabic precise. "Still the careful guardian of things best left undisturbed."

El-Amin's jaw tightened. Tara could see a flicker of fury in his eyes; the indignation of a scholar whose life's work was being casually dismissed by a man with a piece of paper and a private army. "This site is under the authority of the International Archaeology Agency."

The man tilted his head slightly, as though indulging a student. "Not anymore."

He produced a folded document from his shirt pocket and extended it between two fingers. "Emergency authorization from the Ministry of Antiquities. Effective immediately, this excavation is secured under government order."

El-Amin didn't take it. His eyes stayed locked on the man.

"If the Ministry wanted control," El-Amin said carefully, "they would have come themselves."

The man's smile widened, but only a fraction. "You may believe what you wish. I stand here under full authority."

He flicked his hand once. Two of his guards moved without hesitation, stepping to either side of El-Amin.

Tara shifted slightly, instinctively, but the man's gaze found her. For a moment, his expression softened, polite but unreadable.

"You and your colleague," he said, glancing briefly at Alex, "will accompany Dr. El-Amin. Guests, of course. Until I have finished my work here."

Alex opened his mouth, then thought better of it when one of the guards angled a rifle toward the ground between his boots. The message was clear: the conversation was over.

The man in white let the silence hang. Then, almost as an afterthought, he added, "My name is Alaric Moreau. This will go smoothly if you allow it."

He gave a final nod, and the guards gestured them toward the northern line of tents.

Tara didn't resist. Alex followed, shoulders squared, hands loose at his sides. Neither was searched. No hands patted down jackets or boots. The guards seemed confident enough in their numbers and weapons that suspicion wasn't necessary.

El-Amin walked ahead, steps firm but slow. He didn't look back at Moreau.

As Tara crossed the sand, she risked a glance over her shoulder. Moreau hadn't moved. He stood at the edge of the shaft, hands still folded behind his back, staring down into the darkness as though it were waiting for him.

The guards herded them across the camp without a word. Boots pressed sand, rifles hung loose, but their meaning was clear enough.

El-Amin walked ahead, his shoulders back. Tara kept her stride even, eyes scanning the camp. Alex trailed a half step behind, his jaw tight but his hands loose at his sides. No one lifted a hand to help. The workers had melted into the shadows, heads down, pretending they hadn't seen anything. Their fear was a tangible thing, thicker than the dust in the air.

The north tent was waiting, its canvas pale and patched, the flap tied with frayed cord. One of the guards pulled it aside. "Inside."

El-Amin didn't hesitate. Tara followed him in, Alex bringing up the rear.

The space was bare: a cot, a rickety table, and two crates stacked against the wall. The heat pressed in heavily, carrying with it the tang of canvas and dust. The flap dropped closed and their escort's footsteps faded as he retreated to the dig site. Silence returned.

Alex crouched by the crates, rapped his knuckles against the wood. "Empty," he muttered.

El-Amin sat on the cot, elbows on his knees. His face was blank; his eyes locked on nothing.

Tara stood near the wall, pressing one palm against the seam. It was stitched tight; no way out without drawing attention. She shifted her weight, feeling the pistol snug against her ankle. Still there. Still hope.

Minutes stretched, broken only by the hum of activity outside; cases dropped, voices clipped and steady, a generator coughing to life. The camp was changing hands, and no one was pretending otherwise.

Finally, Alex broke the quiet. "He's not here for the pottery."

El-Amin's eyes lifted at that. A faint nod. "No."

"That paper he waved around?" Alex went on. "Forged."

"Of course," El-Amin said. His voice was dry, stripped down. "But he doesn't need it. He has men. He has guns. That is enough."

Tara studied him. "You know him."

El-Amin didn't answer right away. Then: "By reputation. Rumors in the academic underground spoke of him; a phantom who moved between unsanctioned digs in Syria, lost temples in the Amazon—and now he's here. He doesn't discover things, he collects them, and then erases the sites from history, appearing when things are uncovered that should stay buried. Never before. Only after."

Alex leaned back against the crates, folding his arms. "Convenient."

"Calculated," El-Amin said.

Outside, Moreau's voice carried faintly through the canvas—low, calm, precise. It was impossible to catch the words, but the tone was enough. He was orchestrating, not arguing.

Tara moved to the cot, lowering her voice. "If he takes control of the shaft, he'll open it."

El-Amin's eyes flicked to hers, sharp now. "Yes."

"And if the stories are true?" she asked.

For the first time, something flickered in his expression. Not fear. Not yet. But memory. "Then he won't find what he expects."

Alex rubbed a hand over his jaw, watching the flap where light slipped through at the seams. "So we wait?"

Tara shook her head. "We get ready."

She didn't say more. She didn't need to.

Alex shifted his boot, feeling the weight of the pistol holstered tight against his ankle. A faint smile ghosted across his mouth.

El-Amin caught it. His brows lifted slightly. Then, for the first time since Moreau's arrival, he exhaled something close to relief.

"Good," he said. "At least the desert hasn't taken everything from us."

The generator outside settled into a steady hum, low and constant, vibrating through the ground beneath the tent. It drowned out the wind, filling the silence with an artificial heartbeat.

Shadows shifted across the canvas walls as men moved back and forth, carrying crates and equipment toward the shaft. No shouting. No wasted words. Moreau's men knew their work and didn't need to bark it.

El-Amin leaned forward on the cot, listening with his head tilted slightly, his face unreadable. Tara watched him for a moment, then crossed to the narrow slit of light near the center pole. She angled her eye to it, careful not to be seen.

Two guards stood a few yards away, rifles cradled, their posture relaxed but ready. Beyond them, she caught a glimpse of Moreau—his white shirt stark against the sand as he bent over a map laid on a crate. His voice was calm, almost conversational, but every man around him listened as if the words carried more weight than orders.

She pulled back.

"He's planning something," she said.

Alex adjusted his position against the crates, one boot stretched out, the other pulled in close. He tugged lightly at the laces, as if testing them. "Feels like he's done this before."

"He has," El-Amin said quietly. "Not here. Other places. Other sites. Always the same pattern."

Tara kept her gaze on him. "And what happens when he opens it?"

El-Amin's hands tightened, fingers lacing together. He didn't answer.

The flap stirred suddenly, the shadow of a figure blotted the light. One of the guards ducked in, his rifle across his chest. He gave the interior a quick glance, then spoke a single word in Arabic: "Quiet?"

El-Amin nodded once. "Quiet."

The guard lingered half a second longer, then slipped back out. The flap dropped again, canvas rustling as it settled.

Alex smirked faintly. "We're making friends already."

Tara shot him a look, but he only lifted his shoulders. Humor, for him, was armor.

Outside, Moreau's voice rose again, clearer this time. "Carefully. The supports are old. We don't need the shaft collapsing before we've even begun."

Tara felt the words like a stone in her stomach. He was moving fast. Too fast.

She turned back to El-Amin. "We can't stay in here while he takes it apart."

His gaze lifted to hers; dark and steady. "You intend to stop him?"

"Yes," she said. No hesitation.

El-Amin studied her for a beat, then nodded once, as though confirming something he'd already suspected.

Alex leaned forward, resting his forearms on his knees. "We'll need a distraction. Something that pulls the guards away without blowing our cover."

Tara's eyes drifted to the crates. "Lantern oil. There has to be some."

"Controlled fire," El-Amin murmured. "Enough smoke, they'll be forced to check. Not enough to trap us in here."

Alex tapped his boot against the ground. "And once we're out?"

Tara looked between them. "We stay close. We stay quiet. And we see what he's really after before he gets it."

El-Amin gave a slow nod. "Then we'll need timing. Moreau won't leave the shaft. But his men will. Find the seam, you slip through."

The hum of the generator deepened, a metallic rattle carrying through the canvas. Voices rose in response, not panicked, but focused—another order given, another task underway.

Alex shifted again, testing the weight at his ankle. He gave Tara a quick glance, and she caught the flicker of steel in his eyes. A pistol wasn't much against half a dozen rifles, but it was something.

"We don't get a second chance," he said.

Tara answered with a nod. She didn't bother with words.

El-Amin leaned back against the cot, exhaling slowly, as though letting the heat soak into his bones. But his eyes stayed sharp. "Moreau believes he's walking toward power. He's walking toward something else."

Outside, a hammer struck metal. The sound rang out sharply, echoing across the plateau, and the camp shifted around it.

The first step into the tomb had begun.

The tent pressed closer with every minute. Heat clung to the canvas walls, trapping the air inside until every breath felt recycled. Outside, the camp moved to a rhythm that wasn't theirs anymore— boots crossing sand, crates being dragged, and the steady cough of the generator pulsing beneath it all.

Tara crouched near the slit of light again, watching in fragments. Moreau hadn't gone far from the shaft. He stood at its edge like a conductor, his white shirt bright against the gloom, his voice carrying low and calm. The men leaned in when he spoke, moving at his pace, not their own.

She let the canvas fall back. "He's already running the camp."

El-Amin sat forward on the cot, hands clasped loosely between his knees. "He was running it the moment he stepped out of that vehicle."

Alex rubbed at the back of his neck, restless energy in every line of him. "Then we're wasting time sitting here."

El-Amin gave him a sharp look. "You step out now; you don't make it three feet."

Tara didn't argue. She knew he was right. The guards outside weren't careless. They were patient. Waiting.

But every hammer strike from the shaft carried deeper into her chest. She'd heard the sound before—metal bracing stone, scaffolding biting into rock. It meant progress. It meant Moreau was already inside.

She turned back to the others. "We can't stop him from in here. If he opens that chamber…"

Her words trailed off; but they didn't need finishing.

El-Amin leaned back, his shoulders brushing the canvas. For the first time since they'd been locked in, his composure faltered. Not panic—just a flicker of memory, of something he hadn't said.

"You saw what happened when we touched the stone," he said. His voice was low, flat. "The energy in that chamber—it wasn't symbolic. It wasn't ritual. It was built to hold."

Alex frowned. "Hold what?"

El-Amin's eyes fixed on him. "Whatever answers when you break the seal."

The tent fell silent.

Outside, Moreau's voice lifted again. "Steady there. Reinforce the line before you descend."

The words were faint, but they cut sharp enough.

Tara shifted, the pistol pressing against her ankle as she moved. She felt its weight, its promise, its limit. A gun was leverage, not salvation. But it was something Moreau hadn't accounted for.

She caught Alex's glance, saw the same thought mirrored in his eyes. He gave the faintest nod.

El-Amin noticed. His gaze flicked between them, then down toward their boots. A small exhale escaped him, the barest smile touching the corner of his mouth. "Good," he murmured. "At least we're not empty-handed."

The generator coughed again, belching exhaust that drifted

under the canvas. It clung to the stale air, sour in the back of the throat. Tara swallowed against it, forcing her focus tighter.

"We can't wait for him to make the next move," she said. "If he gets further into that shaft, we'll lose any chance."

Alex tapped the toe of his boot against the dirt, restless. "So we make the first one."

El-Amin straightened, resolve settling back into his posture. "Then we make it count. Not noise. Not panic. A clean distraction. Enough to pull them off balance."

Tara nodded once. "Agreed."

The flap stirred suddenly. One of the guards stepped in just enough to glance around. His rifle stayed slung, his expression flat, but his eyes swept the tent quickly before landing on El-Amin.

"All quiet," El-Amin said.

The guard waited a beat, then ducked back out.

Tara listened to the footsteps retreat, then turned back to the others. Her voice was calm, certain. "We're not waiting for morning. We make our move tonight."

Alex leaned forward, elbows on his knees, a grin ghosting across his face despite the heat. "Now that sounds more like it."

El-Amin's eyes narrowed slightly, not with doubt, but with measure. "Then plan quickly. We won't get a second chance."

Outside, a hammer struck stone again, ringing through the camp like a warning bell.

Tara's jaw tightened. Whatever waited beneath them, Moreau was one step closer to it. And unless they acted, he would be the one to claim it.

6

The generator held the camp in a steady drone, a low note that sat in the chest. It swallowed the wind and filled the spaces between footsteps outside. Somewhere beyond the canvas, men moved with quiet purpose. No hammering. No chisels. The shaft mouth had been wrapped earlier in sheets of clear plastic, taped and weighted so dust couldn't drift back into the camp. Whatever they were doing, they were doing it clean.

Inside the north tent, heat pressed close. The air smelled of old canvas and kerosene. Tara stood near the center pole, eyes on the seams, counting the breaths between patrols. Alex waited by the crates, one hand resting on the lid as if it were a starting block. El-Amin sat forward on the cot, elbows on his knees, listening like a man measuring distance by sound.

"Same pattern as before," Tara said quietly. "Two guards pass every couple of minutes. One lingers; one circles."

Alex nodded. "Then we give them a reason to linger."

El-Amin's gaze flicked to the lantern on the table. The glass was cloudy, the handle warm to the touch. "Oil first," he said. "Cot second. We want smoke, not flame."

Tara crossed to the lantern, tested the weight, then turned the knob. The wick was short but sound. She lifted the globe, pinched the wick between her fingers, and felt the tack of oil. Enough.

Alex eased the crate lid open. Empty. He slid the splintered panel free and angled it near the ground between cot and table. "We keep it low," he said. "Let the smoke build where they can't see it right away." His movements were economical and silent, the practiced motions of a man who had gotten out of tight spots before.

Tara set the lantern on the floor and fed the wick a small twist. She touched a match to it. The flame took at once, small but steady. She let it burn long enough for the glass to warm, then blew it out and lowered the globe. A thread of smoke rose, thin at first, then thicker.

El-Amin dragged the cot two steps, careful with the legs, and set it so the canvas would make a pocket. He tugged a blanket half off the mattress and let it drape near the lantern's heat, but not touching. Smoke curled under the fabric and pooled.

They waited. The silence in the tent was absolute now; a shared, held breath.

Outside, the generator dipped and caught again. Boots passed. Voices murmured low. No one paused.

The smoke found the seam at the base of the wall and began to escape in a faint gray line. Tara watched it slide along the floor like a living thing, then rise in a slow ribbon. The tent took on a new smell. Not just kerosene. Burnt cloth. The kind of scent that wakes people before the flames do.

Alex coughed once, a quiet test. He shot Tara a look. She gave him a small nod.

El-Amin checked the flap's tie. The cord was frayed; easy to pull when the time came. He straightened and met their eyes. "When they open it, I will call for water. Alex, you stumble first. Tara, hug the wall and go left. The shadows are deeper there."

Tara flexed her ankle and felt the pistol snug against her skin. A last confirmation. She breathed out and let the breath go soft, like laying a glass on a table.

The smoke thickened, curling upward into the pocket they had made. In the dim light, it was hard to see until it wasn't. The air took on a haze. The canvas above them darkened a shade.

Footsteps approached. One set stopped just outside. The patrol's rhythm had shifted by a beat.

The flap stirred. A shadow fell across the seam.

"Quiet?" came the guard's voice.

El-Amin stayed seated, his tone ironed flat. "Smoke."

The flap didn't move.

Alex coughed harder, bending at the waist, a hand on the crate as if he needed it to stay upright. "It's building," he said, voice rough. Not a shout. Just loud enough to carry.

The guard hesitated, then tugged the flap loose and stepped inside. Rifle across his chest, eyes sweeping the space, he caught the scent and saw the thin column rising from the floor pocket.

"Out," he said, tipping his chin toward the door. No panic. Procedure. He was a soldier, not an investigator, and a smoking lantern was a simple problem with a simple solution in his mind.

El-Amin stood slowly. "We need water."

The guard turned his head and called something short to the second man outside. Another set of boots faded away at a jog.

"Now," Tara whispered, not with her voice but with her eyes.

Alex made it look clumsy. He moved first and clipped the crate with his hip, sending it skittering just enough to make the scene feel real. He coughed into the crook of his arm and stepped past the guard as if grateful to be told what to do.

The guard tracked him, a half-step of attention. Enough.

Tara slid along the wall, left hand brushing the canvas, her body tight to the seam. The smoke helped. So did the guard's focus on Alex. She reached the edge of the flap and slipped through the narrow angle where light broke. The world outside hit hard and bright. She kept low, turned left, and vanished into the narrow throat between this tent and the next.

El-Amin stalled. He crouched and pinched the lantern wick through the glass with a quick practiced motion, starving the smoke before it could become flame. The guard's eyes flicked down to follow his hand.

The second guard returned with a dented water can. Alex reached for it, still coughing, and the man shoved it against his chest. In the distraction, El-Amin moved through the flap with the water bearer's shoulder shielding him for a heartbeat. He peeled right instead of left, breaking line of sight behind a stack of folded tarps.

Inside the tent, the first guard dragged the cot away from the warm pocket, saw that nothing was burning, and swore under his breath without sound. He pulled the flap wide to clear the air. When he turned back, he counted one, two.

Not three.

They regrouped in the narrow space between tents, close enough to hear one another breathe. Tara raised a finger for stillness. The patrol passed again, slower this time, the first guard irritated in that quiet way men get when something small has taken time they didn't plan to give.

Tara leaned closer. "We keep to the shadows," she said. "Crates to the trucks. Trucks to the scaffold. No running."

They stayed low and let the camp move around them. From the seam between two tents, Tara watched the patterns settle into a rhythm. Patrols drifted in loops. A pair held by the generator. Another pair near the vehicles. Two more floated close to the shaft, eyes on the plastic skin that sealed the opening.

Heat rose off the ground in thin waves that made distances bend. Men in gloves eased a frame across the mouth of the shaft, clamping it to the scaffold with precise turns of a wrench. No chatter. No wasted motion.

"Left," Tara whispered.

They slid along the tent line. Canvas brushed her shoulder. Sand whispered under their boots. The generator's drone filled the world and hid small sounds if you timed your steps with it. El-Amin set the pace with that in mind, moving when it growled deepest, pausing when it caught. Each step was a negotiation with the desert floor; a careful transfer of weight to avoid a loose stone or a loud crunch of gravel.

From here the view opened. Three black cases lay open near the scaffold. Their foam interiors were cut to fit specific shapes: polished plates wrapped in cloth, narrow rods, clamps with fine teeth. The plates weren't steel. They were dark and glassy. Obsidian, Tara thought. Edges so clean they ate the light.

Alex leaned close enough for breath to touch her ear. "Mirrors," he said.

"Not for light," El-Amin murmured. "For sound."

Moreau stood at the plastic, speaking quietly to a technician who wore a respirator and a hooded visor. The man nodded, then fitted a hose to a port that had been cut and sealed into the plastic sheet. When he flicked a switch on the small machine at his feet, the sheet drew tight over the scaffold like a drumhead. Negative pressure, Tara realized. Keep dust in. Keep air one way. Moreau watched the first pull, then held up a hand. The plastic smoothed, tolerances exact, and no slack at the seams.

He wanted control. Not theater. Tara's chest tightened. This wasn't a looter's show.

They slipped along the vehicle's flank and reached a run of stacked water cans. From here the shaft looked close enough to touch. A cable winch hummed as they tested a single descent line. The line was new, the carabiners polished. Moreau paced the edge, his white shirt steady, the scarf settled against his throat. He didn't look up at the sun or down at the dust, only at the way his men obeyed when his fingers dropped.

"Timing," El-Amin said softly. "He'll wait for the light to turn."

The breeze had slackened. Shadows shortened and grew heavy. A runner came from the far side of camp with a tablet and showed Moreau something on the screen. He studied it, then nodded once. The runner left and was replaced by a man carrying a canvas roll. He unfastened it on the hood of a truck. Tools gleamed in a row, their shapes unfamiliar. A small set of tuning forks lay in a fitted nest at one end.

Moreau picked up one fork and struck it gently against the truck's frame. The note was soft, thin, almost lost in the drone. He tilted his head, listening. Then he chose a smaller one and did the same. He looked at the shaft. The tech on the hose nodded. Tara felt the hair lift on her arms.

They shifted again, trading the water cans for a deeper seam between a tent and a pallet of wooden crates stamped with a private foundation's mark. She scanned the lettering on the side: Resonance Kit.

Moreau lifted a hand. "Five minutes," he said. The words were quiet, but they traveled.

A guard peeled away from his loop and came straight toward their new hiding spot. Tara watched his boots kick up small puffs of sand with each step; a steady, rhythmic advance that felt as inevitable as a ticking clock. She sank lower, her breath held. The guard stopped on the other side of the pallet and exchanged words with a second man. They talked about water, not suspects. The first cursed softly, turned, and went the other way.

Alex let his breath slip between his teeth.

Moreau had moved closer to the plastic. A man cut a slim slit near the bottom and slid a measuring probe through. Numbers blinked on a handheld. Satisfied, Moreau stepped back and took his first real look at the camp since his arrival. His gaze moved from the vehicles to the tents to the crates. It passed over the seam where they hid and continued, unhurried, unemotional. A man in command surveying a board before the next move.

He raised his hand again. "Hold positions." He turned to the nearest guard. "Bring me the smaller case."

The guard returned with a compact box. Inside, nestled in foam, lay a heart-shaped stone the color of night water, so polished it drew the light down into itself. Moreau looked at it for a long breath as if confirming a promise. Then he closed the lid. "Not yet," he said, and checked his watch.

Tara looked at the sun, then back to the plastic. The air had gone from moving to held. The camp seemed to lean in toward the mouth of the earth.

"He goes at dusk," El-Amin's voice barely carried.

"Then we go before him," Tara nodded.

The choice had been moving toward them since the first vehicle crested the ridge. Across the camp, a patrol changed direction. One guard lifted his chin, scanning the tent line. His eyes narrowed. His course adjusted by a few degrees and he started toward the seam where they hid.

Tara's hand found Alex's sleeve. She pressed once. The signal was clear.

Now or not at all.

7

The guard adjusted course with that small, deadly certainty of a man who'd spotted something. His head angled, his eyes narrowing, and the rifle strap creaked against his vest as he shortened the distance.

Tara sank lower behind the crate stack, back pressed to the rough wood. She held her breath. The scent of dust and oil filled her nose, the desert pressing in close. Beside her, Alex stayed stone-still, the only motion a slow rise and fall of his chest. El-Amin crouched on the other side, hands flat to the ground, steady as carved basalt.

The boots came closer. A scuff of sand. A pause. His shadow fell over their hiding place, a sudden blot of darkness that arrived before the man himself.

The guard stopped less than a dozen paces away.

Tara let her eyes drift toward the seam in the crates. Through a sliver, she caught a view of his profile: jaw tight and sweat catching the sun at his temple. He was young, but not green. His weight shifted evenly, his finger near the trigger guard but not inside it. A professional.

He lifted a hand to shield his eyes, scanning the row of tents beyond. His lips moved faintly, speaking into the mic at his collar. The answer came in a soft crackle—words Tara couldn't catch.

The pause stretched. Every second felt like a minute, the drone of the generator a distant, irrelevant noise compared to the sound of her own blood pounding in her ears.

Then he turned his head, just slightly, and looked directly toward the gap between crates and canvas.

Tara's pulse kicked hard. She eased her hand toward her ankle, as slow as sinking sand, fingers brushing the grip of her pistol. Not yet. Not unless she had to. Her mind raced through the tactical calculations: a silent takedown was impossible from this angle, a shot would bring the entire camp down on them in an instant.

The guard's eyes narrowed further. He shifted his stance and took two steps closer.

Alex's jaw flexed. His hand twitched toward his boot, but Tara gave him the smallest shake of her head. If one of them moved too fast now, the entire camp would be upon them.

The guard paused again, head cocked.

A shout carried from the shaft. One of Moreau's men called for a line to be tightened. Metal clinked, the sound bouncing off scaffolding. The guard turned his head at the noise, then back again, caught between duties.

He raised his mic. "North perimeter clear," he said. His voice was steady, untroubled.

But he didn't move away.

Instead, he lingered another five seconds, eyes still sweeping the shadows, rifle loose in his grip. Then—finally—he pivoted, his boots grinding sand as he angled back toward the vehicles.

Tara let her hand fall from the pistol grip. Slowly. Carefully. She swallowed, her throat dry, and exhaled through her nose.

Alex whispered, barely a breath. "Thought he had us."

El-Amin didn't answer. His gaze stayed on the path the guard had taken, as though waiting for him to double back. Only when the man's shadow had vanished behind the nearest SUV did he finally move.

"Not yet," El-Amin murmured. "But he will come again."

They stayed in the seam another long minute, letting the patrol's rhythm re-establish. Voices drifted back toward the shaft. The generator held its drone. The camp exhaled, unaware three fugitives were pressed against its ribs.

Tara shifted just enough to catch the shaft through another gap. Moreau still stood at its edge, hands clasped behind his back. His attention never wavered, not toward the tents, not toward the patrols. Only down.

Whatever waited below, it had him already.

She leaned back, met Alex's eyes, and mouthed a single word. Move.

They slid along the crates, low and slow, inching toward deeper shadow. Each step was measured with the patience of survival, each pause timed to the drone of machinery and the distraction of men at work.

By the time they reached the far edge of the row, the guard who'd nearly caught them was nothing but a dark figure crossing back toward the vehicles, his rifle a sliver against the light.

Tara pressed a hand to the crate, steadying herself. They weren't safe. Not even close. But they were still unseen. Still alive.

And that was enough to keep going.

The patrol's footsteps faded, swallowed by the generator's drone and the dry rattle of plastic around the shaft.

Tara eased forward first, sliding her shoulder along the last crate until the seam opened onto another stretch of shade. Alex followed, quick and low, his weight balanced on the balls of his feet. El-Amin brought up the rear, as careful as a man who knew every step might be counted.

They moved between shadows until the row of SUVs blocked the sun, then paused behind the second vehicle. The black paint radiated heat like an iron stove. Tara caught the faint reflection of herself in the tinted glass—distorted and stretched; the outline of a fugitive instead of an archaeologist.

Alex leaned close. "We're too exposed here."

She didn't disagree. The open ground between the vehicles and the shaft was no more than thirty yards, but patrols crossed it on a loop that left almost no gap. Moreau's men had built their perimeter with care.

El-Amin's eyes narrowed. "He's learned from other digs. He expects interference."

"Not us," Tara said.

Alex gave a thin smile. "Let's keep it that way."

They shifted again, crawling low until they reached the stacked water cans by the camp's edge. From here, the shaft filled their view.

The plastic shimmered, stretched taut, its surface rippling like the skin of a drum. Moreau stood at its edge, one hand behind his back, the other lifted in small, precise gestures. A technician adjusted clamps, another secured cables, and the winch operator tested the descent line again.

Then one of the black crates opened.

Inside, nestled in foam, was another obsidian plate. This one etched—not carved, not inscribed, but etched by something finer than human tools. Lines crossed its surface in a web of geometry that bent the eye. Shapes that almost formed symbols, then dissolved if you stared too long.

El-Amin let out a breath, barely audible. "That's not excavation equipment."

"No," Tara whispered. "That's for something else."

The technician lifted the plate with gloved hands and carried it toward the scaffold. He fitted it against the frame, aligning its edges with care. When he stepped back, the plate caught the light and seemed to absorb it, darkening the entire corner of the shaft.

Alex swore softly under his breath. "He's lining the opening."

"Or unlocking it," El-Amin said. His voice carried a gravity that made Tara's skin crawl.

The hum of the generator deepened as a second machine kicked in. A low vibration ran through the ground, subtle but steady, as though the earth itself had begun to resonate.

Moreau checked his watch again. His calm never wavered.

One of the guards lifted his head suddenly, scanning the camp. His gaze swept past the vehicles and lingered on the water cans. Too close.

Tara froze.

Alex's hand drifted toward his boot.

The guard took a step in their direction. Another. His rifle lowered slightly, not in readiness, but with suspicion.

Then a shout carried from the shaft. A clamp slipped, ringing metal against metal. The guard turned his head, distracted. He muttered into his mic and angled away, cutting back toward the scaffold.

The moment passed.

Tara's breath left her chest in a slow stream. They had seconds, not minutes.

She looked at Alex, then El-Amin. "We can't wait. If he sets them all, we'll never get near that shaft."

Alex nodded once.

El-Amin's eyes stayed on Moreau, unblinking. "Then we move tonight. Before he goes down."

Tara turned back toward the shimmer of the plastic, her jaw tight. Moreau raised his hand again, and another obsidian plate was lifted into position.

The frame around the shaft was becoming something else—an opening, a gate.

The vibration in the ground deepened, faint but undeniable. The desert itself seemed to lean toward the sound.

And in that moment, as Tara watched the last of the sunlight slant across the plateau, she knew—they were almost out of time.

She whispered, "We make our move before dusk."

But even as she said it, Moreau's head turned. His eyes swept the camp, sharp and deliberate, pausing a fraction longer on the row of vehicles and the shadows behind them.

For the first time, it felt less like they were watching him, and more like he was watching them.

8

As the desert air cooled, it grew unnaturally still, as if holding its breath for what was to come. Heat that had pressed down all afternoon began to lift, bleeding out of the sand in soft waves. The color of the plateau shifted from pale gold to something cooler, the sky deepening toward violet. The air held a different edge now—not gentler, but sharper, as if night had a purpose of its own.

The camp adjusted with it. Lanterns flared one by one, their light harsh against the darkening canvas. A generator coughed, then roared, feeding floodlights that pointed toward the shaft. Their beams cut hard cones across the ground, erasing the shadows in some places and thickening them in others. The men moved faster, more deliberate, aware that night work left no margin for error.

Tara crouched in the narrow throat between two stacks of crates, her back pressed to rough wood. The smell of oil and rope was strong here, but the shadows were deep, and that was all that mattered. Alex was just to her right, watching the patrol rhythm with the patience of a hunter. El-Amin crouched low, breathing steadily, his eyes fixed on the shaft.

They'd slipped closer during the changeover, timing each move with the drone of the machines. Now they were near enough to see Moreau clearly, his white shirt stark against the dark scaffold. He hadn't slowed once since arriving. If anything, the fading light seemed to drive him harder.

Tara's gaze followed his hand as he lifted it slightly, giving a signal with nothing more than two fingers. Men peeled back the plastic that had sealed the shaft all afternoon. The sheets fluttered in the breeze, catching the floodlights like glass. When they came free, the opening yawned wide again, framed now by the obsidian plates bolted into the scaffolding.

It looked less like an excavation and more like an altar.

Alex leaned close enough that his shoulder brushed hers. "He's not waiting."

Tara shook her head. "He's going down now."

El-Amin's voice was low, almost a growl. "He should wait. The stone was sealed for a reason."

"Moreau doesn't strike me as the patient type," Alex said.

Ahead, Moreau stepped onto the platform. He moved with the same calm as when he first arrived—never hurried, never loud. One of his men carried a harness forward. Moreau shrugged it on as if it were a dinner jacket, the buckles snapping home with practiced ease.

A line was clipped to the front. Another to his belt. He checked neither. He simply lifted his chin, and two more of his men adjusted the winch until the cable hummed.

Tara's stomach tightened. He was really going down. All her training, all her instincts, screamed at her to intervene, to do something before he crossed the threshold. But El-Amin was right. Acting blindly now would only get them killed. No probes. No cameras. No hesitation. Just Moreau and the men who followed his hand signals like scripture.

"Arrogant," Alex murmured.

"Certain," El-Amin corrected. His eyes didn't leave the scaffold. "There's a difference."

Tara watched the guards shift as the operation changed tempo. Two moved closer to the shaft, rifles slung across their backs while they worked the lines. Another pair adjusted positions along the camp perimeter, tightening the circle. Every man here had been drilled for this. No slack. No gaps.

Except the shadows.

The floodlights left pockets of darkness thick enough to slip through if you timed it right. That was their only advantage.

Tara tapped Alex's arm lightly, then pointed toward the power unit driving the winch. A small bank of dials glowed there, guarded only loosely. "If we can reach it—"

Alex's eyes narrowed. "We could cut the line."

El-Amin shook his head. "Not yet. He'll be watching. Sabotage now will cost us before we understand what he's really after. I have seen men like him before. They do not seek treasure. They seek a source. If you destroy the path, you may unleash the destination."

Tara clenched her jaw. He was right, but every second felt wasted. Moreau was already stepping into the unknown, and once he was below, there'd be no easy way to stop him.

The winch groaned as tension pulled on the cable. Metal sang against metal, and the first descent began.

Floodlights sharpened. The plastic snapped in the breeze like warning drums.

Moreau's boots hit the edge of the scaffold. He didn't look down. He didn't even glance back at the men watching him. He simply raised his hand again, and the cable whined, lowering him into the shaft.

His men followed, one after another, clipped in and silent. Their rifles slung, their eyes fixed on the darkness below.

Tara's heart hammered. This wasn't an excavation. This was an invasion.

El-Amin whispered, "When he reaches the chamber, the voices will come again."

Tara felt her throat tighten. She remembered the way El-Amin had described it, the sound that wasn't airflow or vibration but something alive, something that had spoken his name.

She forced her focus back. They were too close to panic now.

Alex scanned the perimeter again. "We need a plan before he comes back up. If he comes back up."

Tara nodded. Her voice was flat. "Then we get closer."

The ground trembled faintly with the winch's weight, the cable unspooling into the earth. Moreau was gone from sight now, swallowed by the shaft. His men disappeared after him, their helmets bobbing until the darkness erased them completely.

Only the guards remained. And they were watching everything.

One of them turned his head suddenly, scanning toward the row of crates where they hid. His eyes lingered longer than they should have.

Tara stilled.

The guard angled closer, his rifle loose in his hands, his eyes cutting across the camp with deliberate precision. Not a man on a casual sweep. This one was sharper. Slower. Suspicious.

Tara pressed herself against the crate, shoulders tight, feeling every inch of shadow wrap around her. The smell of oil and canvas filled her nose. Sweat ran down her spine in a slow trail, cold against skin that should have been burning in the desert air.

Alex shifted just enough to bring his boot into contact with hers. She glanced at him. His eyes flicked down, then back up—a question she didn't want to answer. Do we take him out now?

Her hand brushed the pistol at her ankle. One quick shot, and the problem would be solved. But then the whole camp would be on them in seconds.

El-Amin crouched lower, his hand flat to the ground like a man listening through the earth itself. His whisper was barely a sound: "Wait."

The guard stopped five paces from their position. He scanned the seam of darkness between crates and tent wall. His head tilted, lips moving into the mic clipped to his collar.

Tara couldn't hear the words, but she caught the change in his body. His shoulders eased. His weight shifted back onto his heels. Whatever he'd been told, it was enough to keep him from raising the rifle.

But he didn't leave.

He crouched suddenly, one hand sweeping across the dirt as if checking for prints.

Tara's pulse spiked.

Alex's jaw tightened. He adjusted his foot slightly, ready to spring if the man leaned too far in.

El-Amin touched his sleeve lightly, an anchor to keep him still.

The guard's fingers brushed sand into his palm. He stared at it for a moment, then let it spill back in a thin trickle. He straightened, his head turning toward the shaft again. For a long second, Tara thought he'd move on.

Then his gaze snapped back.

Straight toward the shadow where they crouched.

His eyes narrowed.

Tara held her breath.

Another voice called out from the shaft—a command, clipped and sharp. Floodlights shifted, and the guard turned his head. For an instant, the shadow deepened, covering them fully.

He adjusted his rifle strap and started walking, angling back toward the scaffold.

Tara exhaled silently, the release leaving her lightheaded.

Alex leaned close, his whisper edged with relief. "That was too close."

"Next time," El-Amin said, "he won't walk away."

Tara nodded. He was right. They couldn't count on shadows saving them twice.

At the shaft, the winch groaned under new weight. The cable trembled, taut and humming, carrying vibrations from the earth itself. The men on the scaffold adjusted their lines, lantern light glinting off the obsidian plates now fully mounted around the opening.

The sight turned Tara's stomach. What had been a simple excavation shaft hours earlier now looked transformed—like a gate designed for something to pass through.

She leaned back against the crate, forcing her voice to stay low. "We won't get another chance. If he reaches the chamber, it's done."

Alex glanced at her, then at the power unit feeding the winch. "We hit the controls; he doesn't come back up."

El-Amin's expression hardened. "We don't know what happens if he stays down there. The chamber may take him. It may take all of us. Better to cut him off before he opens it."

The cable shuddered again, the vibration running up through the scaffold into the metal clamps. The men worked fast; tightening bolts and securing lines.

Tara felt the decision settle like a stone in her chest. There was no waiting. No watching. Moreau had forced their hand.

"We need to move," she said. "Before he comes back up. Before he brings whatever's down there with him."

Alex's smile was grim. "Now you sound like a plan I can live with."

El-Amin didn't smile. His eyes stayed locked on the shaft, dark and steady. "If we live through it."

They shifted deeper into shadow, angling toward the power unit. The patrol patterns had changed now, tighter, closer to the shaft. Every step would be risky.

Tara raised her head just enough to gauge the distance. Twenty yards. Maybe less. But every inch of it was lit by lanterns and cut through with guard loops.

They'd have one chance, and one only.

The cable groaned again, then steadied. Moreau's men held the line, feeding it lower into the earth. The sound was metallic, unnatural, as though the desert itself objected to what was happening.

Tara swallowed hard. Her hand brushed her ankle again, the pistol's weight a cold reassurance.

Then—

The guard who had nearly discovered them broke from his loop. He walked toward the perimeter, then stopped suddenly. His head lifted, scanning again. This time, he wasn't looking at sand or crates. He was looking at shadows.

At them.

His rifle angled up, not fully raised, but enough.

And his eyes locked exactly where they crouched.

9

The guard's rifle came up a fraction, not enough to fire, enough to settle his mind. He saw them now. Not a shape. Not a shadow. People.

Tara moved first. She rose from the crouch and took one quiet step into the light as if she had every right to be there. Her hands were empty. Her face calm. The single bold step did what panic could not. It stole a half second from the man in front of her.

Alex took it. He slid low past Tara's hip, caught the rifle barrel with both hands, and twisted. The guard's finger never reached the trigger. The muzzle jerked skyward. El-Amin stepped in from the left and drove his palm into the man's throat. There was a sickening, soft thud of impact— not enough to crush, just enough to take air and sound—and the guard's eyes went wide with shock and pain. The guard fell back into the tether of his sling. Alex wrenched the weapon free and shoved it down, muzzle to gravel.

The struggle lasted three seconds. No shout. No shot.

The man clawed for breath. Tara stepped in close, caught his vest with one hand, and eased him behind the crates. She put a knee on the strap across his chest and held him there until his eyes cleared.

Then she took the radio from his collar and rolled him to his side so he could breathe.

Alex watched the patrol routes without blinking. He counted to five. Then to ten. No heads turned. No one had seen.

El-Amin leaned close to the guard's ear. His voice was flat. "Sleep now." He pressed a point under the jaw and held it. The man's eyes slipped shut. Not a choke. A pressure that would leave the guard dazed for long minutes.

Tara listened for any change in the camp rhythm. Nothing broke. The generator droned. Lanterns hummed. The winch sang its cold song down in the shaft.

She looked at Alex. He nodded once. They slid back into the shadows and moved.

They took the long way, trading a straight sprint for a lettered path along the tents. They hugged cloth and rope and stacked cans. They crossed a strip of open ground when the floodlight swept in the other direction and the patrol reached the far vehicle. They reached the power bank without drawing a single head.

The winch control stood waist high, boxed in steel. Two thick cables ran from it to the generator. Dials glowed green. A small lever marked Brake sat under a slotted guard.

Alex crouched to study the base. He traced the cable with two fingers and found a bolted panel at his knee. Tara watched the nearest guard. He had his back to them and his mind on the scaffold.

El-Amin knelt beside Alex. He whispered to save breath. "Stall it. Do not kill it. If the line fails, the weight may take the men below."

Alex nodded. He slid the bolted panel free with a short wrench from his pocket. The panel dropped into his palm without sound. Inside, the cables were clean and labeled. He felt the heat in them. The winch pulled hard on its load. He ignored the thrum of power under his fingertips, his entire focus narrowing to the schematics he had memorized from a dozen similar systems.

He counted the lines. Power. Brake. Remote. He found the brake slave line and the power feed that ran the drum. He looked up once at Tara and saw his thought reflected there. Stall. Do not cut.

Tara kept her eyes on the scaffold. Men leaned over the mouth of the earth, feeding cable at a measured pace. A floodlight moved to cover a darker corner. The light flared, then steadied. The plastic that had been peeled back earlier now hung in long flags on two sides, snapping softly in the new breeze.

"Now," she said.

Alex pulled the brake line from its socket and slid it back in halfway. Not enough for a clean contact. Enough to lie. He watched the dial. Nothing changed. He reached for the power feed next and loosened the clamp a quarter turn.

The drum gave a tired hitch and pulled again. The pitch shifted. The cable thrummed. The operator frowned and tapped a gauge with two fingers.

Tara took one step right to block the operator's line of sight. She knelt as if tying a bootlace. Alex turned the clamp a hair more. The dial went from steady green to an amber blink.

The operator looked up, then down, then cursed quietly and tapped the gauge again. He leaned to his right and called something toward the generator. A man at the fuel line lifted his shoulders. Everything looked normal from his angle. The operator glanced toward the scaffold. He did not panic. He did not call a halt. He did what a steady man does. He watched. He tried the line again.

Alex gave the clamp a final turn and set the brake line fully home. He reached up and flipped the safety cover on the brake lever without moving it.

The drum shivered. The cable paid out an inch more than it should, then caught.

Far below, in the black column of air, a shout kicked up the line and reached them as a ghost. The men on the scaffold peered down. One adjusted his pulley with a gloved hand. The operator tightened his jaw and fed the line slowly.

The winch shuddered again and steadied.

Tara exhaled. She did not smile. That small struggle in the machine told her what she needed. There was grit in the gears now. If they had to, they could freeze it in place. One pull and the brake would slam home. The drum would lock. The line would hold.

She pressed a finger to the brake lever without moving it. She let herself imagine Moreau at the end of that line. Then she let the thought go. Not yet.

Guards shifted near the scaffold. The man who had almost found them earlier returned from his loop, saw the operator's frown, and walked over. He leaned in and asked a quiet question. The operator tapped the gauge. The guard looked into the shaft. The cable hummed. The guard gave a small nod and stayed close.

El-Amin watched the camp without moving his head. "We have one chance," he said. "We freeze the drum and hold the line. Then we decide if we cut it or take it back."

Alex lifted an eyebrow. "Cut it while he is down there and we cannot know what the chamber will do."

"We do not cut," Tara said. "We hold him where he cannot move and we go down."

Both men looked at her. She let the plan sit in the air and waited for either of them to argue. Neither did.

"There is a second line on the far side," she said. "Backup. We clip to that and drop fast while they are still trying to figure out why the drum froze. We reach him before he reaches the chamber. We pull him out or we stop him below."

El-Amin's gaze was steady. "And if the voices begin."

"Then we do not listen," she said. "Headphones if we find any. If not, we go by touch."

Alex's mouth tightened. "I like simple plans."

"They are the only ones that work," Tara said.

A ripple of motion moved through the men near the scaffold. Someone below called up. The operator leaned over and shouted back. Words lost in engine noise. The guard lifted his mic. The reply was clipped and fast.

Tara looked at the dial. The amber blink held steady. She reached for the brake.

"On my count," she said. "Three. Two. One."

She pulled. The lever came down with a clean, irreversible feel.

The drum screamed once and locked. The entire scaffold jolted. The cable went rigid. Every man on the platform threw a hand to a line or a brace. The guard grabbed the rail and swore under his breath. The operator reached for the lever and found Tara's hand there already. She pushed him back with her shoulder; all quiet force.

Shouts rose from below. This time they were not ghosts. They rode the cable, the air, and the metal, and came out harsh.

The camp turned its face toward the shaft.

The nearest guard swung his rifle around. He did not lift it high. He aimed it at the machine and the people near it. He saw a woman with a steady hand on the emergency brake, a man at the panel he did not know, and an older man who did not look away from the dark hole in the earth.

He opened his mouth to speak.

Alex pointed past him and shouted, "Line!" in a voice that sounded like one of theirs. The operator turned his head on reflex. So did the guard. The winch man looked down. The guard leaned.

Tara stepped past both and reached for the backup line coiled on a hook. She bled it free with a snap, clipped it to her harness with a motion that had no hesitation, and tossed the rest of it across the platform toward the second anchor.

El-Amin moved with her. He took the second clip and fed it through the ring with hands that had learned knots before most men learn sums. Alex swung the panel closed and shoved the brake cover back into place in case anyone looked too closely. He slung the captured rifle and stepped to the line.

The operator saw what they were doing half a second too late. He reached for the brake to free it. Alex caught his wrist and closed fingers on tendons. The operator froze, not from pain, from surprise at a hand that did not belong to his crew.

The guard swung the rifle back toward them.

Tara drew the pistol from her ankle and held it low against her thigh where only the man in front of her could see it. She did not point it at his chest. She pointed it at the winch. She shook her head once.

The guard hesitated. He understood machines. He understood what a bullet to a casing under load could do. He saw the cold certainty in her eyes and made a split-second calculation, weighing his duty against the lives of the men suspended hundreds of feet below.

"Stand down," Tara said. "You have men on that line."

The guard's jaw worked. He did not like being told anything by a stranger, especially a woman. He liked killing a machine while his people hung from it even less. The barrel dipped. Not a lot. Just enough.

"Go," El-Amin said.

They went.

Tara stepped to the edge, took the spare line in both hands, and dropped into the throat of the shaft before any other thought could get between her and the dark. The first fall was six feet of slack, then the line caught her harness. Her breath left and returned. She braced boots against stone and eased the friction knot with her right hand. The world narrowed to rope, rock and breath, and the drum hum in her bones.

Alex came after her. He moved fast and sure. He did not look up. He did not look down. He matched her pace because that is what he did in every difficult situation they had shared.

El-Amin followed with the steady weight of a man who accepted gravity as part of the bargain. His hands did not shake as he fed himself down the line in short clean moves.

Above, the guard shouted. Another man lunged for the brake. The operator fought for his controls. Their voices tangled. None of it reached the three figures that dropped into the earth.

For a time there was only the rope, the black and the scrape of boot on stone. The floodlights from the rim cut the first twenty feet. After that, the light thinned, then failed, and the shaft swallowed it whole.

The temperature changed. Cool air rose up the column. It

smelled of stone and old water and metal that had not seen the sky in a thousand years. It was a dead, sterile cold that had nothing to do with the desert night above and everything to do with the sunless depths. The sound changed too. The drone of machines turned to a skin-deep tremor and then fell away. The rope hummed like a live wire against their harness rings.

Tara counted her breaths. She counted the pace of her hands on the line. She kept her mind on the next move and no other.

A smear of light drifted below. A headlamp. Then another. Voices floated up the shaft in a language that had no home. Quiet syllables. It might have been one man speaking to another. It might have been the abyss speaking to itself.

Tara did not listen. She pressed the headphone cups from her pocket against her ears and slid them on. No noise cancelling in the world would silence what had spoken to El-Amin. The mufflers would blunt the edges. That was enough.

Below, the first platform came into view. Moreau's men had affixed a temporary stance there, a brace for gear. It was empty now. The real descent continued past it. Light hung in beads along the main line. It ran into a cut that led to the chamber. She felt it before she saw it. A pressure at the base of the skull. The same wrongness she had tasted in Iceland. The same near-pulse in the stone.

She reached the platform and waited for Alex. When his boots hit metal, she caught his harness and steadied him. El-Amin came next. They did not speak. They leaned out and looked down.

A larger light bloomed below. Not a flood. A steady glow that was not theirs. Not lantern. Not headlamp. It had the slow pulse of a heartbeat trained to a metronome.

Moreau's voice rose through the column. Calm and clear. It touched the metal, the rope and their bones as it drifted up to them without wind.

"Nearly there," he said.

Another voice answered. It did not belong to any man.

Tara shut her eyes. It did not help. The sound had weight. It pressed at the soft edges of memory. It did not say her name. It did

not need to. It touched the shape of her thoughts and searched for a
seam.

El-Amin reached across the gap and pressed his palm to her
shoulder. The touch anchored her. He lifted the small device he had
carried from the camp. Not a tool. A relic. A shard of lead plate he
had wrapped in cloth and slipped into his shirt the day the chamber
first spoke. He held it toward the voice that was not a voice.

The pressure eased a fraction. Not much, but enough to breathe.

Alex leaned over the edge and peered down to the next drop. He
counted the clips on the main line and mapped their descent in his
head. He touched the second rope. It was true. The anchors on their
side were old, but solid. The weight they carried was theirs alone.

Above, a floodlight shifted. Voices argued. Men moved. Someone
had finally understood what they had done to the brake. Someone
had pulled a radio and called for orders. Those orders would bring
men to the rim with rifles very soon.

Tara looked at El-Amin. He nodded. She looked at Alex. He
grinned without humor. They pushed off the platform together and
dropped the next stretch in near silence.

The shaft widened and the stone changed. It went from rough to
smooth and from honest to something like intent. The walls bore a
polish that was not decorative. It felt like a surface made to carry
sound along it. The rope vibrated with the same low tone that had
nothing to do with machines.

They reached the lip of the chamber.

It opened like a mouth into the hillside. The floor sloped toward a
central slab. The air moved, not with wind, but with a slow convec-
tion of temperature as if something below was colder than any air
had a right to be. Obsidian plates lined the entrance in a pattern that
was both random and designed. Some of them were new—Moreau
had placed those—others were older than any of them could name.

Tara crouched behind a stone rib and looked in.

Moreau stood ten yards from the slab. His harness hung loose
now. He had unhooked himself from the line and trusted the
chamber with his back. He looked smaller down here. He did not

move like a man who had found limits. He moved like a man who thought he had been welcomed.

Two of his men flanked him. One held a coil of cable, the other held a case—the case Tara had seen on the truck hood. The box that had held an obsidian heart that drank light.

It lay open at the man's feet.

The heart sat in its nest and pulsed with that slow impossible glow. Tara's breath hitched. It was the same object from Iceland, or a twin to it. The same impossible geometry, the same light-devouring presence. The nightmare she thought they'd left behind in the ice was here, waiting for them in the sand.

The sound that was not a sound grew richer. It did not come from the heart. It came from the stone around it. It collected on the walls like breath on glass.

Moreau lifted a hand and the men stopped moving. He spoke without turning his head. "Do you hear it," he asked, "or do you feel it."

Neither man answered. They did not need to. He did not expect it. The question had not been for them.

Tara eased backward and met Alex's eyes. They did not have time to think in long lines. They had seconds. The camp above would be in motion. The men below would see them if they crossed the mouth in the wrong second.

El-Amin pressed the shard of lead against the wall. The tone shifted, but did not break. The wall took that small defiance and folded it back into itself like a river takes a stone.

He looked at Tara. His voice was almost nothing. "Mirrors," he said. "Obsidian for sound, lead for silence."

Alex nodded. He did not know the science. He knew the intuition. He pointed to the old plates and held up three fingers. He pointed to the new plates and held up two. An improvised count of what was theirs and what was Moreau's.

Tara set her jaw. She slid the pistol into the strap at her waist so both hands were free. She pulled a coil of cord from her belt and looped it around a newer plate near the mouth. She tested the knot once. Then she eased it tighter.

If the plates fed resonance into the chamber, one broken angle might break the feed. One cracked note might ruin a song.

She did not look at Moreau again. She kept her eyes on her hands and the plate at her fingers. She kept her mind on the knot and the angle of the pull.

Alex watched the men in the chamber. When both turned their heads toward Moreau, he slid to the second new plate. He worked faster than was wise. He could not help it. He had a clock in his blood when danger pressed. The knot bit. He tested it once. He pulled.

The plate did not move. It had been clamped and sealed. He bled force into the line instead. A wedge of wood in his pocket went under the cord to spread the torque. He leaned his weight into it and felt the mount complain.

A voice behind them said, "Hold where you are."

It was not Moreau. It was a guard who had followed the line down and found the platform, then stepped into the mouth as silent as a cat.

Tara did not turn. Alex did. He saw the man at the edge. The muzzle aimed at Tara's spine. He saw the bullet that would go through her and the plate, and all the plans they had left.

He let go of the cord with his right hand and reached for his boot.

The guard took one step closer. His finger settled.

A new sound rolled through the chamber. Not the tone they had been riding, a deeper cut. The heart in the case flared once like a coal fed new air.

Moreau turned his head toward the mouth where they crouched. He did not flinch at the sight of them. He smiled as if greeting old friends he had expected. Then he lifted his hand and pointed at Tara.

"Bring her," he said.

The guard took a second step.

Alex's pistol cleared his ankle holster and came up in one clean line. The floodlights above flickered. The brake on the drum screamed as someone finally forced it free.

The main line jerked and paid out two feet.

Moreau's head lifted, not in alarm, in recognition. Something below the slab answered the change. The tone in the walls swelled as if pleased. The guard's finger tightened.

Tara pulled on the cord.

The obsidian plate snapped free with a sound like glass losing its will. A discordant shriek echoed through the chamber as the carefully constructed resonance field collapsed in on itself. The chamber went dark and bright all at once.

And the voice that had not yet said her name found it.

10

The chamber breathed in slow intervals, a cold exhale that slid over skin and found the spaces between heartbeats. It was a palpable presence, a living architecture that responded to them in ways that defied physics. The light here didn't behave like light. It pooled. It gathered along the polished stone like water seeking a hollow.

They kept to the chamber's edge, a rib of stone that rose waist high. Beyond it, the floor sloped toward the central slab and the open case at its foot. Inside the case lay the obsidian heart, a black geometry that drank the glow around it and gave back a pulse—soft, then softer still, as if learning how to be seen.

Moreau stood ten yards out, harness unclipped, hands empty. He faced the slab without moving and spoke in a voice that belonged to a room where everyone had already agreed to listen.

"You were buried by men who feared truth," he said, almost gently. El-Amin flinched, a barely perceptible tightening of his shoulders. To him, this was not a man communing with the past; it was a zealot attempting to awaken a nightmare. "I am not afraid."

No one answered. Not the men to his left or right. Not the wall.

Not the heart. But the chamber itself shifted, like an instrument tuned a fraction, and a new note slipped through the stone.

Tara eased closer to the rib and let her palm hover a hair above the polished surface. The vibration was there—faint, like a moth beating against glass. She moved her hand toward one of the dark plates lining the mouth. The note sharpened. She pulled back toward a lead patch stamped with shallow glyphs. The note blurred and fell apart.

Obsidian carried. Lead broke. She mouthed the words to Alex. He nodded once, eyes never leaving Moreau.

El-Amin kept the shard of lead against the wall near his hip, as if holding a small breach open. His face had the stillness of a man praying and refusing to call it prayer.

Moreau's men shifted their weight but tried not to. They were brave enough to follow him down a rope into an old throat of stone, but courage had a calibration. The heart adjusted its breath and the men adjusted theirs with it, and the room took note of which of them matched its pace without meaning to.

"Prepare it," Moreau said.

The man to his right knelt at the case. He drew back the padded lid and carefully unrolled a series of cloth pouches. Inside lay tools that didn't look forged so much as grown—slender implements of bone and metal, a narrow set of tongs with pads of leather at the tips, a small ring whose inner edge had been inlaid with hairline grooves. He handled them as if a wrong thought might chip them.

Tara had seen meticulous operators before—conservators who treated paint like breath, divers who set charges the size of a thumb and spoke to stone through water. This was different. The tools weren't for fixing or breaking. They were for coaxing, the way a tuning fork coaxes a room into agreement.

The heart's glow gathered on its cut planes and then collapsed inward, like a throat that had considered speaking and decided to wait. It didn't reflect anything. It showed the room what it felt like to look at it.

"Listen," Moreau said quietly. "Listen and do not fear it."

His men tried. The one with the tongs swallowed and set the pads against a lower edge, careful not to touch the surface itself. The leather kissed the stone with a sound too soft to be heard and too loud to be ignored.

The note in the wall changed again.

It wasn't language. Words would have been easier to resist. This was pitch and memory braided together; a music that looked for old doors inside the mind. It brushed the shape of a name and moved on. It tested a childhood sound and moved on. It looked for a seam. For a fraction of a second, Tara felt the phantom warmth of a sun on her face from a memory that wasn't hers, a sun that hung green in a purple sky.

Tara slid the muffs tighter over her ears. The world dulled. The note found her anyway, felt for the border between thought and reflex, and pressed there with the patience of dripping water. She pressed the side of her head to the cold rib and let the lead shard near El-Amin's hand share its refusal with her bones.

Moreau took one step closer to the slab. He lifted his hands a few inches, palms forward, as if greeting an old friend who had never once spoken to anyone uninvited.

"Those who sealed you lacked the will to finish what they began," he said. "They made a cage and called it reverence. I bring release."

The chamber held its breath and then let it out as a long, slow tone that did not belong to air. It touched the spine. It smoothed the muscles along the jaw. It found the hinge in the ear where heartbeat meets echo and set up a tent there.

Alex's fingers tightened white on the edge of the rib. He didn't look at Tara. He didn't look at El-Amin. He kept his eyes on Moreau and let the room test his quiet.

El-Amin's mouth moved with a word he did not say aloud. His thumb worried the edge of the lead, a tiny motion in a place that made even tiny motions feel like arguments.

Tara pointed—two quick taps—toward a newer obsidian plate Moreau's team had mounted near the mouth. The cut wasn't perfect; they'd forced it into an older slot. Sound pooled there like water behind a crooked stone. If they cracked that angle, they could make this instrument stutter.

Alex followed the line of her finger, tracked the way the tone strengthened along that edge, and gave a single nod.

The man at the case lifted the ring with a grooved interior and held it over the heart. Moreau didn't touch a single tool. He watched, statue-still, as if his presence alone were his part and anything more would be vulgar.

"Slow," he said softly. "Let it answer."

The ring lowered. For an instant, the grooves aligned with the cut faces and the heart brightened, not outward, but down into itself. The glow turned from cold to something like embers buried under ash.

Tara felt the note lift at the edges of hearing and then step down, lower than before. It grew heavy. It rolled through the stone, up through the rib, into her hands. It asked nothing. It assumed. The room would agree because agreeing would be easier.

Her fingers drifted toward the cord she'd tied to a plate at the mouth. She stopped herself. Not yet. The room wanted reaction. It fed on it. It would take any move and call it call-and-response. She needed the wrong move, the kind that didn't fit the rhythm the chamber set.

Moreau's head tilted. He breathed in through his nose as if the room had offered him a scent he had spent years trying to remember. "Yes," he said, more to himself than anyone else. "There you are."

The man with the ring swallowed. His hands didn't shake, but his eyes shone with the effort of not letting them. He set the ring gently on its cradle beside the heart and reached for the tongs again.

"Enough," Moreau said. "It knows."

He turned his head fractionally, just enough that his profile cut against the glow. The look he gave the chamber wasn't triumph. It was recognition. The ease of a man who had finally arrived at the room he had always believed existed.

Tara felt it then, something small but precise, as if the note narrowed to the width of a needle and touched the space a breath in front of her face. Not her name. The idea of her. A mapping of edges. The room finding a shape and considering whether it fit.

She slid lower behind the rib and let the lead shard's refusal carry through her shoulder into her chest. El-Amin glanced at her and read the change in her eyes. He pressed the shard into her palm without a word.

The heart pulsed again. The ring of grooves drank and gave the pulse back, one fraction out of phase, a deliberate imperfection built to keep the song from closing fully. Whoever had designed this had understood that perfect agreement is surrender.

Tara let the knowledge settle. Not a theory. A plan waiting for a moment.

Across the floor, Moreau lowered his hands. The smile that touched his mouth was small and real. He had not conquered anything yet. He believed he was being acknowledged.

"Bring the second case," he said.

His men moved.

The second case came forward, carried by Moreau's lieutenant— the same hard-eyed man who'd nearly discovered them in the camp above. His face was cut from discipline, lean and humorless, and he carried the case not as if it were fragile but as if it were dangerous.

He set it down beside the first, kneeling so Moreau could flip the latches himself. The clicks echoed too loud in the chamber. Each one sharpened the tone that already lived in the walls.

Tara ducked lower behind the stone rib, the lead shard warm in her palm now, almost eager. She traded a glance with Alex. His eyes said what hers were already thinking: If that man looks this way, it's over.

Moreau bent, unhurried. He lifted the lid. Inside, wrapped in linen darkened by centuries, lay another object—smaller than the heart but shaped with the same unnatural geometry. Not a sphere, not a cube, but something in between, a form designed to catch the mind in its corners.

The glow from the first heart bled toward it, thin streams of light dragging across the air like mist reaching for water. The new object drank it, and for a moment the chamber dimmed.

Moreau breathed out in wonder. "Twins," he whispered. "Separated, hidden, and now—home."

The tone deepened.

The lieutenant rose and turned half a step, scanning the chamber mouth with a soldier's instinct. His eyes narrowed. He had the look of a man whose suspicion wasn't an arrow but a net—patient, ready to tighten. He began walking.

Tara pressed her back flat against the stone. Alex's hand closed on her forearm; to steady, not restrain. El-Amin clutched his side of the rib, the lines of his face carved deep with fear held in check.

The man drew closer, boots whispering against the smoothed floor. He carried no lantern, yet the walls painted light across his profile. He reached the rib at the mouth and paused, his rifle angled low, eyes narrowing into the shadows.

Every muscle in Tara's body went still.

Alex moved his hand toward a loose stone near his knee. He pinched it between two fingers, silent as breath, and flicked it out into the chamber. It rolled three feet, struck a wall, and bounced once before vanishing into the slope.

The sound was nothing. A pebble's accident.

But the chamber magnified it. The tone shifted in reply, feeding the small knock into its echo until it seemed to have come from deep within the heart itself. A hollow answer.

The lieutenant jerked his head toward the sound, his body taut. He lifted the rifle, aiming past the slab and into the deeper darkness.

Moreau didn't turn, he simply said, "Ignore it."

The words cracked like a whip.

The man froze, his jaw flexing, and lowered the weapon a fraction. His eyes lingered on the chamber's mouth though, sharp as knives searching for a sheath.

Tara barely breathed. She had been hunted before, by men, by weather, by places that wanted her gone, but this felt different. It wasn't just the man, it was the chamber. It wanted her to move, to twitch, to cough, so it could carry the sound straight to him.

The lieutenant's gaze lingered a moment too long. Then Moreau's voice cut through again, soft but absolute. "Here. Now."

The man turned. His boots carried him back to the slab. He didn't hesitate, but his back was stiff, his shoulders locked.

El-Amin let out a breath as slow as a prayer.

Tara's pulse rattled, but her hands steadied. She leaned closer to Alex and whispered against his ear, the words barely a sound. "Not fanatics. Cracks showing."

He gave a single nod, the kind that meant: We can use that.

Back by the slab, Moreau had both objects open now. The glow stretched between them in a thin strand, and the chamber's tone bent again—lower, heavier, pressing into marrow. The men shifted uneasily. One of them muttered something sharp in French, fear edging his tone.

Moreau turned his head slightly, and the man fell silent at once.

But Tara had seen it, the way the chamber unsettled them more than their commander did. They were soldiers, trained and paid. But they weren't blind zealots. They were men standing in a place where stone itself hummed with hunger.

The lieutenant crouched again by Moreau's side, but his eyes darted once more toward the chamber mouth, like a man who couldn't shake the sense that the dark was watching back.

Alex's whisper brushed Tara's ear. "That one will break first."

She didn't argue. She only gripped the shard of lead tighter and felt the way the tone hated it.

The heart pulsed. The twin answered. And the chamber prepared itself for something none of them understood.

The strand of light between the two black geometries thickened, no longer mist but something closer to molten glass, alive with slow movement. It quivered as if testing its own strength, then held fast.

The chamber shuddered with it. A deeper tone rolled across the walls, steady and exact, vibrating in Tara's teeth. She clamped her jaw, but the sound wasn't in her ears, it was inside bone; a current that knew the shape of marrow.

Moreau raised both hands, not like a priest but like a man welcoming his own reflection. His voice was calm, reverent. "At last."

He turned slightly, enough for his words to reach his men. "Do you understand? This is no curse. No fable. This is resonance itself—the voice beneath the world. It doesn't speak in words. It speaks in truth. With it, kingdoms rose. With it, they feared collapse."

The lieutenant said nothing. His jaw held tight.

Another man, the one who had handled the tools, shook his head faintly. Sweat stood out on his temples. "Monsieur... this is wrong. It should not be touched."

Moreau pivoted, his eyes as sharp as glass. "Touched? You think this is a thing you touch? You think it stone, or jewel? It is thought given form. Those who buried it tried to silence the truth itself. They failed. They always fail."

The man's breathing quickened. He backed away a step from the case, palms out. The glow from the linked artifacts brightened as if noticing him.

The chamber's tone swelled. He flinched. His rifle clattered to the floor, echoing like a thunderclap. He turned and ran toward the rope.

Tara tensed, her heart leaping. She thought he might make it, might scramble up and break the fragile hold Moreau had over his men. But he never reached the rope.

Halfway across the slope, the sound cut sharply, a single note that spiked like a blade. The man cried out and fell to his knees, clutching his head. The cry ended almost as soon as it began, choked off into a wet gurgle as blood trickled from his ears and nose. He pitched forward, motionless.

The chamber swallowed the silence that followed.

Moreau didn't move. His gaze stayed fixed on the twin artifacts, as if the man's collapse had only confirmed what he already knew. "It chooses," he said softly. "It knows the weak. It knows the unworthy."

His eyes gleamed with a dangerous certainty. "And it knows me."

Tara's grip on the lead shard bit into her palm. She could taste metal on her tongue though she hadn't bitten it. She forced herself to keep low, to stay unseen. But the room was restless now. The glow didn't stay tethered between the two objects. Thin threads peeled away, spider-silk strands wandering out toward the chamber's edges.

One of them drifted toward her. She pressed herself flatter against the rib. Alex's hand tightened on her wrist. El-Amin touched the shard with two fingers, steadying her grip.

The strand curved, following her shape like a heat signature. It was not just light; it was an inquiry, a tendril of ancient consciousness that mapped her bones, tasted her fear, and sifted through her thoughts with terrifying intimacy. She thought of the way El-Amin had described it back in the tent—the whisper that said his name. This was worse. This didn't need words. It knew.

Her pulse thundered. The lead warmed further, fighting. But the thread didn't pull back. It hovered an inch from her shoulder; a needle of light quivering, tasting the seam between her and the stone.

Alex leaned close, his whisper as sharp as a blade. "I think it sees you."

The words shouldn't have chilled her more than the glow already did—but they did. Because she felt it too. The sound shifted again, and for the first time it wasn't just vibration, it was suggestion. Shapes in a memory. Not hers alone—something older trying to make her believe they were hers.

The desert at night. A river flashing with torchlight. A crowd bowing in silence as a slab closed over something too bright to be borne.

None of it hers. Yet the chamber tried to press it into her bones as if memory were nothing more than clay.

Tara shut her eyes tight, clutching the shard of lead to her chest. The weight of it steadied her heartbeat, cut one thread of the false vision. The rest tried to cling.

A low laugh drifted across the chamber. She opened her eyes. Moreau was looking straight at her.

Not shocked. Not surprised. Calm, inevitable, as if this moment had been written in a book he'd already read. His eyes met hers, and in them she saw something terrible—recognition. He lifted his hand, pointing not at the slab, not at the artifact, but at her.

"You see it," he said. His voice carried, wrapped in resonance. "It answers you."

Every head in the chamber turned. Soldiers shifted, their eyes widening. The lieutenant's grip on his rifle tightened, suspicion dark in his stare, but he didn't raise it. Not yet.

Tara's breath locked in her chest.

The strand of light that had found her brightened, sharp as a drawn blade. The chamber's tone bent with it, as if the ancient voice had turned to face her alone.

And Moreau's smile, slow, thin, and certain, made clear what he believed.

"It has chosen," he whispered.

11

Every man standing near the slab had turned toward her, their eyes reflecting the faint glow spilling off the artifact. No one spoke. The only sound was the low, steady thrum of resonance in the stone, a sound that wasn't sound at all but something that clung to muscle and marrow. It was a silence filled with a terrible, unspoken question.

Tara didn't move. She forced her features into calm neutrality, though her pulse was hammering a frantic rhythm against her ribs. Alex shifted subtly closer, his presence brushing her shoulder, a quiet reminder that she wasn't alone. El-Amin crouched low against the rib of stone, his gaze fixed not on Moreau but on the soldiers.

Moreau broke the silence first. He stepped toward the slab, his hands slightly lifted, palms open as though the glow were something fragile that could be frightened away. "You all felt it," he said quietly, but the chamber carried the words across every surface. "It isn't chance. It isn't accident. The resonance recognizes her."

The soldiers exchanged uneasy looks. Some leaned forward, drawn in by the conviction in his voice. Others shifted back a fraction, unsettled.

Tara found her voice. Calm. Even. "Or maybe it's just showing you what you want to see."

The words echoed oddly, bouncing from one obsidian plate to the next until the chamber itself seemed to consider them.

Moreau's head tilted slightly. He studied her the way a predator studies prey that doesn't run. "No," he said. "It shows truth. And truth has no concern for what we want."

His certainty pressed down harder than his words. Tara knew there'd be no reasoning with him. Men like Moreau didn't come here to be persuaded otherwise. They came to bend the world to their will and called it destiny.

The lieutenant moved then—the same soldier whose suspicion had nearly caught them above ground. His sharp and measuring gaze never left Tara. "Monsieur," he said, voice low but firm, "with respect... if it recognizes her, what does that mean for us?"

The question carried weight. It wasn't curiosity. It was fear.

Moreau didn't so much as blink. "It means we stand at the edge of history. That every man in this chamber will be remembered for being here when the world shifted."

The soldiers glanced at one another. They wanted to believe. But wanting and believing were not the same thing.

Alex leaned his head just enough toward Tara that his whisper barely touched her ear. "He's losing them."

Tara's eyes flicked sideways. El-Amin had heard it too. His jaw tightened, his thumb brushing the edge of the lead shard hidden in his hand. He didn't speak, but the intent was clear—press the cracks, widen them.

Moreau stepped closer to the slab, his voice rising slightly. Not loud. Controlled. "You've seen what happens to the unworthy." His eyes flicked toward the body of the soldier who had tried to flee, still sprawled near the rope. "Weakness is punished. Fear is punished. But those who accept the truth are elevated."

The lieutenant's jaw flexed. He didn't argue, but he didn't nod either.

Tara used the moment. "He wasn't weak," she said, her voice steady. "He was smart enough to know when to walk away."

That drew every eye again. The chamber seemed to like her words—the tone swelled, a low vibration in the ribs of stone.

Moreau's face hardened. "Smart?" He gestured toward the fallen man. "He died running from what he should have embraced. There's no wisdom in that. Only failure."

He turned his gaze back to her, sharp as a blade. "But you—you won't fail. You were drawn here for a reason."

The words pressed like a verdict, but Tara met them without flinching. "If I was drawn here, maybe it was to stop you."

The tension snapped taut. The soldiers muttered, some shifting uncomfortably, others gripping rifles a little tighter. The lieutenant's eyes flicked between Moreau and Tara, the conflict plain on his face.

Alex stepped forward half a pace, putting himself slightly in front of Tara. His voice was quiet but hard as stone. "You'll have to go through me first."

Moreau studied him, not amused now. For a moment his mask of calm cracked, and Tara saw what lay beneath it—a fiery obsession unwilling to be denied. But just as quickly, he smoothed it back into control.

"You misunderstand," he said. "This isn't about going through anyone. It's about what she is meant to do."

He raised a hand toward the slab. The glow pulsed, responding to the gesture like a trained animal. "Step forward," he indicated to Tara. "The chamber will decide."

The soldiers waited, tense and silent. The lieutenant's rifle dipped slightly, not quite aimed not quite at rest.

Tara's pulse thundered. She knew stepping forward meant surrendering control. But refusing would trigger something just as dangerous. Either way, the ground was giving way beneath them.

She glanced at Alex. His jaw tightened, a silent promise: Whatever happens, we move together.

El-Amin's eyes burned in the half light. His lips pressed into a line, his silence heavier than words.

Moreau's hand remained outstretched. "Now."

Tara didn't move. She held her ground behind the rib of stone, the glow from the slab painting her cheek in cold light.

Alex shifted a half step more in front of her, his stance low, balanced. His hand brushed the hem of his jacket where the pistol rode hidden at his ankle. Not yet—but close.

El-Amin rose from his crouch. Not quickly. Not defiantly. Just enough to stand, hands open, his eyes scanning the soldiers rather than Moreau.

"No one here doubts your conviction, Monsieur Moreau," he said, his voice calm, almost weary. "But you saw what happened to your man. The resonance punished him. You think it chose him unworthy? Perhaps. But consider this—what will it do when you force someone to step forward against their will?"

The words weren't aimed at Moreau. They were aimed at his men.

A ripple went through the group. One of the soldiers tightened his grip on his rifle. Another glanced down at the fallen body near the rope. Even the lieutenant's eyes flickered with something. Doubt? Or calculation?

Moreau's head turned slowly toward El-Amin. "You speak like a man who has spent too long in the company of tomb dust. Fear dresses itself in reason, but it is still fear. The resonance does not punish. It refines. Those who falter are cast aside. Those who endure are transformed."

El-Amin didn't flinch. "Transformed into what? A shell? A corpse? You think power is given freely. It never is. It takes. Always more than you expect."

The chamber thrummed at his words, the walls vibrating with a low, unsettling tone. The soldiers shifted uneasily again. The glow from the artifacts pulsed, brighter now, as if the very stones enjoyed the tension.

Moreau stepped closer to the slab, his expression hardening. "You mistake your role here, Doctor. You were useful once. You uncovered what others feared. But now—" He gestured at Tara. "Now the chamber reveals the true path. You cannot change that by hiding behind warnings."

His eyes turned back to Tara. "Step forward. You don't need to fear it. It already knows you."

Tara felt the weight of his stare like a hand pressing against her chest. She forced her voice to calm. "If it knows me, then it doesn't need me to prove anything."

The lieutenant's head turned sharply at that, eyes narrowing. It was a clever deflection, and he knew it.

Moreau's jaw flexed. "You speak like someone who doesn't yet understand. The resonance has no patience for games." He lifted his hand higher. The glow surged in answer. "Every second you delay, it grows stronger. Do you feel it?"

Tara didn't answer. She wouldn't give him the satisfaction. But she did feel it—every bone in her body hummed with an unnatural frequency, as if her blood itself had learned a rhythm it didn't want.

El-Amin broke in again, louder now, but still addressing the men. "You've followed him down here, into a place that shouldn't have been opened. You've felt it. In your teeth. In your bones. Tell me— how long before it takes you too?"

One of the younger soldiers swore under his breath, a sharp syllable that carried fear. Another spat on the ground, a nervous habit. The lieutenant barked something short in French—an order to hold position—but even his voice was tight.

Moreau's patience frayed. "Enough." His voice cracked like a whip, sharp enough to still the chamber's muttering. "You think doubt protects you? It only weakens you. And weakness—" He pointed at the dead man again. "—is already rotting at our feet."

His arm swung back toward Tara. "Bring her."

Two soldiers moved immediately, rifles snapping up as they stepped forward. Their faces were pale, jaws clenched, but they obeyed.

Alex shifted in front of her fully now, his stance braced. His hand hovered just above the pistol at his ankle, waiting for the first sign of necessity.

El-Amin didn't back down. He spread his arms slightly, placing himself at Tara's side, blocking half the path to her. His voice stayed low, but firm enough that the men could hear it. "You've seen it punish. You haven't seen it reward. Ask yourself—why not? Why hasn't it blessed him yet?"

The question landed.

The soldiers hesitated mid-step. One faltered enough to glance at Moreau.

Moreau's face hardened into something dangerous; obsession burning past patience. "Because the time is not yet right," he said through clenched teeth. "But it will be. When she steps forward, when she surrenders to it, the resonance will open fully."

Tara's chest tightened, but she kept her eyes on him, steady and unflinching. "Maybe that's exactly what it wants, Moreau. Not to give you power. To feed on you. To feed on all of us."

The chamber responded with a pulse so strongly the floor trembled under their boots. Even Moreau's men looked rattled. The lieutenant's jaw worked. He barked another order, but his tone lacked the sharp confidence it had before.

Alex leaned closer to Tara without taking his eyes off the soldiers. "It's breaking. He's pushing too hard."

She nodded faintly. But the rifles stayed aimed. And Moreau's eyes stayed locked on her.

His voice dropped—quiet and deadly certain. "You will step forward. One way or another."

Two soldiers advanced, rifles raised. Their boots scuffed against the polished stone, the sound magnified by the chamber until it seemed louder than it should have been.

Alex stepped in front of Tara, blocking their path. He stood square, shoulders tight, every line of his body warning them to stop.

"Not one more step," he said. His voice was low, controlled, but it carried.

The men hesitated. Not because of him, but because of the chamber. The glow from the twin artifacts brightened again, throwing their faces into stark relief. They looked pale, sweat beading on their temples.

Moreau spread his hands in mock patience. "Do you really think you can hold her back forever? This is larger than all of us."

"No," Alex said. "It isn't. It's just you, forcing everyone else to play along with your obsession."

Moreau's smile thinned. "Obsession is a word the powerless use when they see vision they cannot grasp." He turned his head slightly toward the soldiers. "Take her."

The two men moved again, rifles tight against their shoulders.

Alex reacted first. He shoved the nearest rifle barrel upward and drove his shoulder into the man's chest. The soldier stumbled, his shot cracking into the chamber ceiling. The sound tore through the space, unnaturally loud, amplified by the stone until it felt like a blast wave. Dust sifted down. The glow of the artifacts pulsed brighter, answering the violence.

The second soldier lunged, swinging his rifle like a club. Alex twisted, the stock grazing his ribs, and yanked the weapon free. It skittered across the floor.

Chaos broke out.

Two more guards rushed forward, shouting as they closed the distance. El-Amin stepped in front of Tara, arms spread wide. He did not fight, but his presence slowed them, forcing them to maneuver around him. It was enough time for Alex to recover, duck low, and drive a fist into the gut of the nearest man.

The resonance fed on it all. The chamber vibrated with every strike, every shout, every shot that echoed. The twin artifacts glowed with a rhythm that matched the violence, brightening in pulses that seemed to quicken as the fight intensified.

Tara stayed close to the rib of stone, her hand tight on the lead shard. She felt it heating in her palm, repelling the resonance that tried to press into her thoughts. She scanned the chamber; mind racing, calculating. The obsidian plates, the soldiers, the lieutenant who hadn't yet moved. He stood near the slab, rifle half raised, watching with sharp, unsettled eyes.

Moreau never flinched. He stood at the center of it all, calm and commanding, the glow painting him in otherworldly light. His sharp and steady voice cut through the chaos. "Bring her forward. Now."

The words carried more weight than they should have. The resonance seemed to bend around them, amplifying the command. The soldiers stiffened as if compelled.

Alex saw it too. His expression tightened. He grabbed the downed soldier's rifle and swung the butt across another's jaw, dropping him to the floor. "We are not moving," he barked, forcing his voice to carry just as far.

The chamber took that too, the words echoing in defiance. The glow flickered, uncertain, as if it could not decide which command to favor.

The lieutenant stepped forward at last. His rifle leveled at Alex; steady and sure. "Enough," he said. His voice was clipped, firm, the accent cutting each word like steel. His eyes, though, betrayed conflict. "Stand aside."

Alex didn't move. He held his ground, the muzzle inches from his chest. His eyes never left the lieutenant's. "You saw what happened to your man. Do you want the same fate? Because that's where this leads."

For a moment, the chamber seemed to hold still. Even the glow dimmed, as if waiting to see what the lieutenant would choose.

Moreau's expression hardened. "Do not hesitate," he snapped. "She is the key. The chamber demands her."

Tara lifted her chin, her voice steady. "Maybe the chamber isn't demanding. Maybe it's baiting you. Maybe you're exactly the kind of man it feeds on."

That drew another ripple through the men. Doubt, thick and sharp.

The lieutenant's jaw tightened. His rifle wavered. Only slightly, but it was enough.

Moreau's eyes burned, his control slipping. He snapped his hand toward Tara. "Take her!"

The chamber roared.

The twin artifacts flared with a violent pulse, flooding the chamber with blinding light. The floor trembled underfoot, dust fell from the ceiling in thick streams. The resonance rose to a fever pitch, rattling teeth, shaking bones, pressing into minds with crushing force.

Several soldiers staggered back, covering their ears, though it did nothing. One dropped his rifle; his face twisted in panic. Another fell to his knees.

The lieutenant shouted something lost in the din, his voice swallowed by the resonance.

Alex grabbed Tara's arm, pulling her closer, shielding her body with his. El-Amin pressed the lead shard against the wall, trying to break the chamber's grip, but the vibration swallowed even that small defiance.

And then, through the white blaze of light, Moreau's voice carried clear. Strong. Certain.

"Bring her to the slab!"

The soldiers moved again, driven less by will than by the resonance itself, stumbling forward through the brilliance. They moved like puppets, their own fear and survival instincts overridden by the chamber's overwhelming command.

Tara clenched her jaw, her hand wrapped around the shard, and felt the chamber pressing directly into her mind. It wasn't words. It wasn't thought. It was command.

Her knees buckled as the world blurred.

The last thing she saw before the light swallowed everything was Moreau's smile—calm and triumphant—as if the chamber itself had bent to him at last.

12

The light faded, but not all at once. It peeled away in ragged layers, leaving behind afterimages that burned against the dark. The air shivered, filled with heat and dust, and every man in the chamber seemed frozen mid-movement, faces half lit, half shadowed.

Tara blinked hard. Her vision swam. Shapes drifted and re-formed the altar, the slab, the black ribs of stone overhead. The resonance still pulsed, weaker now but erratic, as though the tomb itself was struggling to breathe.

Alex was beside her, one knee down, one arm shielding her from falling debris. "You all right?"

She nodded, though she wasn't sure. The floor trembled once, a slow roll that sent grit sliding toward the center of the chamber.

El-Amin coughed somewhere behind them. "It... stopped?"

"No," Tara said quietly. "It's changing."

Across the chamber, Moreau stood near the slab, the Heart clenched in both hands. The glow no longer filled the space, it clung to him instead, pulsing through his veins like liquid light. His men kept their distance, some staggering, others clutching their heads as if trying to block out a sound no one else could hear.

"Do you see?" Moreau's voice cracked through the dust. "It recognizes me now. It knows who commands it."

He looked radiant and ruined all at once, his eyes fever-bright, his skin glistening with sweat. The air around him warped faintly, bending light as though the world itself had begun to ripple.

Tara felt the resonance crawl over her skin, searching. It wasn't sound, it was pressure, a vibration in her teeth and spine. She forced herself to stand, every muscle trembling. "You can't control it, Moreau. You're feeding it, not mastering it."

He laughed softly, a sound with no humor. "Always the scientist. Still pretending this is something to be measured."

Behind him, one of his soldiers dropped to his knees, blood seeping from his nose. Another stumbled against the wall, leaving a smear of red where his hand slid down polished stone.

El-Amin pointed. "It's rejecting them!"

The soldier convulsed once, then stilled. The resonance wavered. The obsidian plates around the chamber caught the light and threw it in broken shards across the floor, dozens of fractured reflections flickering like ghosts.

Tara's gaze followed the pattern. The reflections overlapped, collided, then folded into each other—light chasing light until the shapes disappeared into a single dark point on the floor. For an instant, the sound dipped low enough that she could hear her own breath again.

And in that silence, she saw it, the Heart's glow bending back on itself whenever it touched one of the mirrored plates. Each reflection twisted the light tighter, compressing it. The Heart didn't like that. She could feel its resistance, the way the energy buckled inward instead of spreading outward.

Moreau raised the artifact higher. The resistance increased, making the glow flicker. He didn't notice. Or maybe he thought it was obeying him.

Alex caught Tara's look. "What is it?"

She didn't answer yet. Her mind was running too fast, calculating angles, remembering the old geometry carved into the walls. Reflection. Refraction. Recursion. Everything here had been built to direct energy, to shape it, to contain it.

The Heart wasn't a source. It was a mirror too, one that amplified what it touched.

She turned toward El-Amin. "The plates, the array, they're still aligned along the chamber's curve?"

He followed her gaze, squinting through the haze. "Mostly. Some cracked, but the sockets remain."

"Then if we angle the light..." She stopped herself, glancing at the soldiers. Not yet.

One of them shouted suddenly, jerking his rifle toward the shadows. "Something moved!"

The others spun, their nerves shattered. The barrel swung past Alex, and he shoved Tara behind a column. A burst of gunfire split the air. The sound ricocheted off the stone, exploding in echoes that multiplied instead of fading. Every shot made the resonance flare, feeding it.

Moreau screamed, not in pain but in rage. "Stop! Do you want to undo everything?"

The men froze. Even the echoes seemed to hesitate before dying away.

Tara leaned out from cover. The Heart's glow was unstable now, flaring too brightly, then fading to near black. She saw small cracks forming along its surface, hairline fractures glowing faintly like molten veins.

"It's destabilizing," she said under her breath.

Alex's face tightened. "Meaning what?"

"Meaning if it collapses on its own, we're all part of the blast radius."

El-Amin crawled closer, his voice low. "Can you stop it?"

"Not stop," she whispered. "Redirect." Her eyes darted to the mirrored plates again. "If we can make it see itself..."

Alex gave a grim nod. "Then it devours its own reflection."

She didn't know how he understood, but he did. He always did.

Moreau turned toward them then, suspicion sharp. "What are you whispering about?"

Tara stood slowly, keeping her hands visible. "You're losing control of it, Moreau. Look at your men."

Two more had collapsed. Another backed away, muttering a prayer in a voice that wasn't quite his own. The resonance slithered between them like invisible smoke.

Moreau's jaw clenched. "They are unworthy vessels. The chamber selects its own."

"No," she said. "The chamber is rejecting you. You're out of alignment."

He barked a laugh that cracked into a cough. The glow around him surged, then dimmed again. "You think you understand this? You can feel the pulse, can't you? It's in you, too. That's why it recognizes you. You were chosen."

The word chosen echoed with a deep harmonic that made the mirrors hum. Cracks spider-webbed through one of the obsidian panels nearest the altar.

Tara stepped closer, forcing calm. "Maybe it recognizes me because I can hear it. Because I can tell it's trying to stop you."

Moreau's expression faltered, just for a heartbeat.

Behind him, the cracked mirror gave a sharp pop and split in two. Both halves caught the glow from the Heart and threw it back at different angles. The light collided mid-air and vanished with a sound like imploding air.

Every man in the chamber flinched.

Tara stared at the spot where the light had died. Her pulse kicked. That was it.

"Alex," she murmured, barely audible, "we need to move those shards. Now."

He didn't ask why. He just shifted, keeping his movements small, sliding toward the fallen plates along the wall.

Moreau's focus was on her again, his eyes wild. "You're trying to distract me."

"No," she said softly. "I'm watching you destroy yourself."

He stepped toward her, the Heart pulsing brighter with every stride. The air thickened and buzzed with energy. The remaining soldiers backed away, uncertain.

Alex eased another shard upright, setting it against a fallen stone. The reflected glow bent, caught the edge of the altar, and curved toward Moreau. He didn't notice—too focused on Tara.

The resonance deepened. It was alive, aware, struggling against its host.

Moreau raised the Heart higher, voice trembling with ecstasy. "It's almost complete. The threshold is opening."

Tara saw the light hit one of the angled shards, bounce to another, and focus directly back toward the Heart. The glow flickered, sputtering once like a candle in the wind.

Moreau faltered, just a breath, confusion flickering through his features. "What—"

Tara felt the pulse skip. The tomb seemed to inhale. Every surface shimmered, waiting.

She held her ground, her voice barely above a whisper. "You think this thing is afraid of us, Moreau? It isn't. It's afraid of itself."

He took another step forward, gripping the Heart tighter. "What are you—"

The light flared again, stronger than before, but this time it curved backward, folding through the mirrors. The reflections multiplied, each one catching a fraction of his image, feeding it into the next until the entire chamber became a maze of mirrored light—one man reflected a hundred times, each one holding the same burning stone.

And for the first time, Moreau looked uncertain.

The resonance stuttered, then rose to a pitch that drilled through bone.

Tara met Alex's eyes across the chamber. No words were needed. The trap had begun to form itself.

13

The tunnel twisted around them like a throat closing. The air thickened with grit and the hiss of falling sand. Tara's lungs burned, every breath laced with dust. Behind them, the sound of the chamber collapsing was constant—stone grinding over stone, a deep groan that came from the bones of the earth itself.

"Keep moving!" Alex shouted, his voice muffled by the noise. He pulled El-Amin ahead, gripping the older man's arm. The doctor stumbled but didn't stop, his left leg dragging from a shallow cut he'd taken earlier.

The light from their headlamps danced wildly across the passage, catching flashes of carvings that hadn't been visible before—spirals, mirrored symbols, and strange humanoid figures with empty eyes. Every reflection from the shattered obsidian fragments scattered along the floor seemed to move with them, slithering like liquid shadow.

Tara reached a junction and hesitated. The right path sloped downward, back toward the resonance chamber. The left angled upward. "This way!" she called, turning toward the faint draft whispering through the rock.

They ran.

The ground pitched again, sending them to their knees. A plume of dust rolled past, blotting out their lights. Tara crawled forward until her fingers brushed smooth stone—the edge of another rib support. She pressed her ear against it and heard the tomb breathing, not metaphorically, but with a slow rhythmic pressure, air pushing in and out of cracks as the structure sealed itself.

"It's closing the passages," she gasped.

El-Amin coughed hard. "Like a living organism sealing a wound."

Alex helped him up. "Then we're escaping through its throat. Let's move before it shuts."

They sprinted as the floor began to tilt upward. The passage narrowed, the ceiling lowering until they were forced to crouch. A deep vibration rolled beneath their feet, then a sharp crack tore through the stone behind them. When Tara looked back, the tunnel's mouth had begun folding in, edges grinding together.

"Go, go, go!" Alex pushed them ahead.

They burst into a larger corridor, one that had once been part of the original excavation route. The metal scaffolding and lamps from Moreau's team still clung to the walls. Most were dark, but a single work light flickered near the ladder shaft leading to the surface.

Tara nearly sobbed at the sight.

They climbed.

Alex went first, steadying the ladder as the others followed. The rungs shook with every impact from the tomb below, each tremor closer than the last. Halfway up, a violent quake hit, throwing El-Amin sideways. His hand slipped. Tara caught his wrist just in time, her knuckles scraping against rusted metal.

"Hold on!" she shouted.

"I've got him!" Alex reached down and hauled El-Amin higher, muscles straining. The older man groaned, but his grip held. Together they climbed the last meters and spilled out into the upper chamber, collapsing onto the packed sand floor.

For a moment none of them moved. The wind from the open shaft above brushed against their faces; cool and unreal. Then the noise started—a low rumble that built until the ground itself seemed to shudder in pain.

El-Amin sat up slowly, his face streaked with gray dust. "Listen."

They did.

Beneath them, the sounds of the tomb were changing. The grinding subsided. The deep, hollow echo softened until it was almost gone. Then, one by one, the vibrations faded completely, replaced by a silence so profound it seemed to absorb the air.

Tara stood and moved to the edge of the shaft. She shone her light down, but the beam went no farther than a few meters before vanishing into darkness. The ladder below them ended abruptly in rock.

"The passage is gone," she said softly. "It resealed."

Alex looked down beside her. "Like it was never there."

El-Amin brushed the dust from his hands, staring into the darkness. "Perhaps that's the point. Containment complete."

Tara swallowed, her throat raw. "And Moreau?"

No one answered right away. The memory of his final scream still hung in the air, half heard, half imagined.

El-Amin exhaled slowly. "I'd say he's gone."

Alex resisted the urge to chuckle. But he certainly didn't feel bad about the demise of the madman.

They gathered what strength they had left and stepped out into the cool night beyond the tomb's mouth. The desert spread before them, endless and pale beneath a thin veil of stars. The storm that had threatened earlier had passed, leaving a stillness that felt unnatural after the chaos below.

Tara turned back. The slope of sand that marked the tomb's entrance looked smooth again, undisturbed, as though the excavation had never happened. Only the half-buried scaffolding and the scattered equipment remained—a graveyard of tools without purpose.

Tara stared at the sand where the shaft had been. She felt the faintest vibration through her boots—a single heartbeat, deep and distant, as if something below was listening. Then it stopped.

Silence settled in. Not the absence of sound, but a deliberate still-ness, as though the earth itself was holding its breath.

Alex broke it softly. "We need to report what happened."

"Not yet," Tara said. "Not until we understand what we unleashed."

El-Amin glanced at her. "You think it's still there, still alive?"

Her eyes lingered on the horizon. "Alive isn't the word," she said. "But nothing that old truly dies. It just waits to be found again."

As they stood there, the wind rose gently, erasing their footprints one by one.

When they finally turned to leave, Tara looked back one last time. The dune where the tomb had been was still. No sound. No pulse. Just sand.

But as the wind shifted, a faint shimmer rippled across the surface, like light glancing off a mirror buried just beneath the skin of the earth.

The wind was wrong.

It carried heat instead of cold, a breath from beneath the sand instead of across it. Tara noticed it first. She had been standing near the slope where the tomb entrance had been, staring at the smooth surface that had sealed itself, when the vibration returned—faint and steady, almost polite. The sound was too low to hear, more felt than sensed, a thrum deep in her bones.

Alex was kneeling beside El-Amin, bandaging a scrape on the older man's arm. He looked up when he saw Tara freeze. "What is it?"

"Listen."

He did. For a moment there was only wind. Then the ground pulsed once, a heartbeat too deliberate to be natural. The sand shifted underfoot.

El-Amin's eyes darkened. "It's not over."

Tara's mind raced. The tomb had sealed, yes, but the resonance had never simply stopped, it had folded inward; compressed, trapped. What if it wasn't dying? What if it was waiting?

A whisper threaded through the air, thin as silk. None of them could make out the words, but the tone was unmistakable: repetition.

"Tara."

The voice was behind her.

She spun, flashlight sweeping the darkness. The desert was empty.

Alex rose slowly. "Tell me you heard that."

"I did," she said. Her mouth was dry.

El-Amin struggled to his feet. "Then the echoes survived."

The sound came again, faint and distorted, carried on the moving air. But this time it wasn't Moreau's voice, not entirely. It was layered, dozens of voices overlapping, repeating fragments of things that had been said inside the tomb. Her own words came back to her: It's afraid of itself.

The desert air shimmered. For a moment Tara thought she saw movement beneath the sand, light shifting just under the surface like the gleam of buried mirrors.

Alex took a step back. "It's resonating through the ground."

"Not just the ground," Tara said. "Through us."

The pressure in her chest deepened. Her heartbeat felt out of rhythm, syncing instead with that low pulse from the earth. She pressed a hand against her sternum, half afraid she would feel it beating under her skin in a pattern that wasn't hers.

The whisper rose again, clearer now. Watson. Return.

El-Amin swore softly in Arabic. "It remembers your name."

Tara forced herself to steady her breathing. "It remembers everything."

The wind shifted again, blowing down the slope. A faint glow bled through the sand, spreading in irregular veins. The light moved like water, tracing the outlines of what had been the tomb's entrance.

Alex grabbed her arm. "We need to leave this area. Now."

"We can't," she said, pulling free. "If it's reactivating, it'll spread. Containment has to hold, or it will echo until it finds another vessel."

He looked at her as though he already knew what she was thinking and hated it. "You're not going back down there."

"There may not be a choice."

The sand cracked like glass. A column of dust shot upward, and with it came sound—a drawn-out hum that rose until it became a scream of feedback. The glow intensified, pushing through the surface in arcs of fractured light.

El-Amin shielded his face. "It's reopening!"

Tara dropped to one knee, staring into the spreading light. "No. It's remembering itself."

The air bent inward. The ground rippled like disturbed water. For one surreal moment, the desert became a mirror. She saw herself, Alex, El-Amin—and behind them, faint but visible, the outline of the chamber taking form through the reflection. The altar. The mirrors. The shadow that had been Moreau.

Alex shouted over the sound. "What are we looking at?"

"The echo," Tara said. "A full harmonic reflection of everything that happened down there."

The images in the mirrored sand flickered. The outline of Moreau moved. His form wavered, almost human, his face a blur of light and shadow. When he spoke, the sound was a chorus, one voice made from many.

"You can't contain truth."

El-Amin took an involuntary step backward. "It's him."

Tara's throat tightened. "No. It's what's left of him. The chamber's consciousness is wearing his shape."

The figure tilted its head. "I showed you what you are."

The light surged upward, coiling around them like threads of smoke.

Tara raised her hand toward the glow, not in defiance but in understanding. "You're not supposed to be free," she said quietly. "You're supposed to stay buried."

The ground responded with a single heavy pulse that knocked them all to their knees. When the light receded again, the mirrored sand had hardened into a glassy crust.

The reflection of the chamber was gone.

But the hum remained.

It beat once more, then split into two distinct tones, one echoing the other, like a voice answering itself.

El-Amin caught his breath. "It's building resonance again. Another cycle."

Tara stood, staring down at the faint shimmer beneath the crusted sand. "Then we go back. If the echo's alive, it'll need a focus point. We can't let it form one."

Alex's face paled. "You mean the Heart's fragments."

She nodded. "If even one piece still resonates, the feedback will start again."

He glanced at the sealed ground. "Then we'd better find a way in before it finishes remembering how."

The wind died completely, leaving them in a silence so pure it felt wrong.

Then, faintly, from somewhere below, came the unmistakable sound of footsteps—slow, deliberate, and far too familiar.

14

The first sound was the sand shifting. A slow drag, deliberate, like something learning how to walk again. The surface bulged and broke, the grains spilling away from a forming shape. A hand emerged first—if it could be called a hand. It was translucent, made of light and dust, its edges trembling with vibration.

Alex aimed his light at it. "You've got to be kidding me."

The glow from beneath intensified, spreading outward in concentric circles. Each pulse threw sand aside until the figure stood fully revealed. It was Moreau's outline but not his body, a specter shaped by memory and resonance. The features were blurred, as if drawn in smoke, but the stance was unmistakable—confident, possessive, certain of command.

Tara felt the air shift as the echo stabilized. The temperature dropped sharply, the same numbing cold she had felt before the Heart first sang. Every sound carried a faint harmonic behind it, a perfect repetition.

El-Amin whispered, "The resonance has rebuilt his pattern. It used him as a vessel before, it's using the memory now."

Tara stepped forward carefully, every instinct telling her to run but knowing retreat wouldn't matter. "It isn't him. It's what the chamber remembers of him."

The echo tilted its head. Its mouth moved, and the voice that came out was layered and wrong. "You can't destroy truth. Only delay its reflection."

Alex muttered under his breath, "That's definitely him."

The apparition turned, its gaze sweeping over them. The light emanating from its body brightened, casting long shadows across the sand. The ground beneath its feet began to vibrate in expanding ripples, turning the surface to liquid glass wherever it passed.

El-Amin gripped Tara's shoulder. "It's re-forming the chamber."

He was right. The dunes around them began to sink, folding inward as if gravity had changed direction. The air thickened with dust that didn't rise but fell in slow spirals. The faint shimmer of the mirrored walls reappeared, not as solid structures but as reflected memory, ghost geometry rebuilding itself in light.

Within seconds, the desert had become the chamber again, its boundaries defined by resonance rather than stone. The altar re-emerged at the center, its surface cracked and glowed faintly from within.

Alex stared in disbelief. "We're inside the echo."

Tara felt it too, the pressure, the vibration under her skin. "No," she said quietly. "It's inside us."

The apparition that wore Moreau's face stepped onto the altar. The air around it shimmered, forming faint spirals that twisted upward like smoke. Its voice deepened until the words came through every surface at once. "You can't trap what mirrors itself."

El-Amin looked to Tara. "He's right. A resonance loop can't end unless it finds something to cancel it."

"Or something to reflect it perfectly," she said. Her eyes darted to the cracked remnants of obsidian scattered across the new floor. "The shards. They're still in play."

Alex frowned. "We used those to collapse the Heart. There's nothing left."

"Maybe not of the artifact," she said. "But the energy still needs surfaces to exist. It's bouncing through us now. If we can redirect it, maybe we can burn it out."

The apparition's head turned toward her. "You understand reflection. But do you understand what it reflects?"

It raised its arm. The air bent. The vibration slammed into them like a physical force, knocking all three to the ground. Tara's ears rang. She looked up to see the ghost's hand extended, palm open, and in its center a faint shard of light hovered—the Heart's fractured core, reborn in memory.

Alex groaned, rolling to his knees. "He's pulling it back together."

Tara forced herself to her feet. "No. It's rebuilding what it thinks the Heart should be. A reflection of the original."

El-Amin pointed. "Then destroy the reflection."

The ground trembled harder. Fragments of obsidian lifted off the floor, spinning in slow arcs around the figure. Each piece caught and magnified the light until the air filled with shards of mirrored energy, all aimed toward the ghost of Moreau.

The hum climbed in pitch. The echo was closing the feedback loop again.

Tara reached for the nearest shard, her hand shaking. The surface burned against her glove, yet when she turned it toward the apparition, the light bent. For an instant she saw not Moreau but herself reflected in its face—pale, exhausted, defiant. The chamber seemed to hesitate.

Alex's voice cut through the noise. "It's working! Whatever you're doing, keep it up!"

She turned the shard slightly, angling it so that the reflection from another fragment struck the apparition's chest. The light intersected, forming a cross of brightness that split its image into twin halves. The echo screamed—a hundred overlapping voices shredding the air.

El-Amin stumbled forward with another shard. "Here! Combine them!"

They moved together, positioning the reflective pieces until they formed a crude circle of light around the apparition. Each mirror caught the same glare and threw it back inward.

The resonance peaked, tearing the ground open in thin fissures that glowed white. The ghost of Moreau staggered, flickering like an old film reel.

"You can't end me," it said, voice breaking apart. "I am every reflection of truth you deny."

Tara's reply was steady. "Then you'll die seeing yourself."

The mirrors flared, converging their light on the hovering shard in the echo's palm. The glow imploded. The figure convulsed, the air filled with a deafening harmonic, and in one moment the entire mirrored world collapsed inward—an echo consuming itself.

When the light died, only silence remained. The desert returned, moonlit and still, the wind whispering softly as if nothing had ever happened.

Tara stood alone for a moment, her vision swimming. Alex and El-Amin were still there, both alive, both staring at the spot where the apparition had vanished.

El-Amin's voice broke the quiet. "Was that the end?"

Tara exhaled slowly. "I think we just gave it what it wanted—a perfect reflection."

The hum beneath the sand faded to nothing. For the first time since entering the tomb, the world was quiet.

But far out across the dunes, a single shimmer of light moved once beneath the surface and disappeared.

The silence after the collapse was fragile, like glass holding its breath.

Tara didn't trust it. She waited, her pulse still hammering in her throat, as the dust settled and the shimmering air calmed to stillness. The dunes around them looked ordinary again, just sand and shadow. But the light that had vanished seconds before began to seep back, faint as starlight bleeding through fog.

Alex noticed it too. "You see that?"

She nodded, already stepping forward. The glow spread across the sand in thin, branching veins, tracing the outline of the altar that shouldn't exist anymore. "It's not gone," she said. "It's resetting."

El-Amin's voice was hoarse. "Residual energy. The resonance doesn't just disappear—it migrates."

Tara crouched and pressed her hand against the ground. The vibration beneath it was softer now, no longer violent but rhythmic. It pulsed once every few seconds, like a fading heartbeat. "It's losing coherence," she murmured. "But if we leave it like this, it'll start echoing again once the cycles stabilize."

Alex took a slow breath. "Then we stop the cycle."

She met his eyes. "We seal it for good."

He looked past her to the horizon. Dawn was just beginning to gray the edges of the sky. "Tell me how."

Tara glanced at the shards of obsidian scattered across the sand. Most were dull now, but a few still carried a faint internal shimmer, like dying embers. She picked one up. Its surface reflected nothing but the glow inside itself. "We can use the pedestal's fragment," she said. "If we align it with the remaining shards, the reflected energy might collapse back into a null field. The resonance will have nowhere left to go."

El-Amin's expression tightened. "A null field that powerful would devour everything near it. Including us."

"I know."

Alex shook his head immediately. "No. We find another way."

"There isn't one," she said softly. "The chamber rebuilt itself once. If it happens again, it won't stop at the tomb."

She looked at the sky, at the faint light of dawn spreading upward, and thought of the voices, the way the resonance had remembered names, faces, moments. It wasn't just an echo. It was memory trying to survive.

Alex read the thought in her face. "You're not staying here."

"I have to."

He stepped closer, dirt and blood streaked down his face. "You said that thing feeds on reflection. If you're in it when it collapses—"

"It will stop," she said, cutting him off gently. "For good."

El-Amin touched her shoulder. "There may be another solution. We can contain it, maybe redirect the energy—"

"There's no time."

The light beneath the sand brightened again, swelling like breath drawn too deep. A faint vibration rippled outward. The dunes began to shift, forming a shallow depression that mirrored the shape of the original chamber.

Tara took the pedestal shard from her pack. It was heavier than it looked, carved from the same impossible stone as the altar itself. Cracks webbed its surface, still glowing faintly from the reflection they had turned inward.

She knelt and pressed the shard into the sand. The hum changed pitch immediately, higher now, resonant enough to make her teeth ache.

El-Amin tried to grab her arm, but the vibration threw him back. "Tara!"

Alex lunged forward, catching her hand. "You can't do this alone."

She squeezed his fingers once, a wordless thank-you. "Then stay with me until it's done."

They worked side by side, dragging the remaining shards into a rough circle around the pedestal fragment. Each piece caught the new light and amplified it until the ring shone like liquid silver. The vibration deepened, turning from hum to heartbeat.

El-Amin shielded his face from the glare. "It's working. The harmonics are aligning."

Tara felt the energy rise through her hands, into her arms, into her chest. The ground beneath them began to sink, the sand melting into glass, sealing over the forming ring. "When the reflections merge," she said, her voice shaking, "the feedback will invert. Once that happens, the echo will have no phase to travel through."

Alex gritted his teeth, struggling against the pull. "Meaning what?"

"Meaning it collapses inward forever."

The wind rose, swirling around them, carrying faint whispers that weren't just sound. Tara heard her own voice among them, repeating things she had said in the tomb—fragments of thought, of fear, of hope. It's afraid of itself. You were never holding it. It's supposed to stay buried.

The words looped around them, tightening, until they weren't echoes at all but commands. The sand flashed white. The circle erupted in light so bright she had to close her eyes.

Alex's hand slipped from hers. The pull was too strong.

"Tara!"

She opened her eyes. The light had expanded, filling the air with sheets of mirrored energy. In its center, where the shard had been, stood the faint outline of the altar, one last reflection of the chamber. And inside it, flickering like a candle in the wind, was the shape of Moreau.

But his face was no longer hateful or triumphant. It was hollow, dissolving.

"You can't bury truth," the echo said, its voice fractured and small.

Tara's reply came without hesitation. "Then you can rest with it."

She turned the final shard toward him. The mirrors aligned.

Light met light.

The sound was indescribable, a note that existed in the body more than the ear. Every vibration in the air folded inward. The reflection collapsed into itself, devouring its own echo, until there was nothing left but a flash like sunrise through crystal.

The ground stilled.

When the light faded, Tara was on her knees. The shards were gone. The sand beneath her hands was cool and unbroken.

Alex stumbled toward her, coughing, his face streaked with tears and dust. "You okay?"

She nodded weakly. "I think it's done."

El-Amin stared at the ground where the altar had been. "No glow. No vibration. It's finished."

The dawn crept higher, painting the dunes in gold. The silence that followed wasn't ominous this time. It was peaceful.

Tara rose slowly, looking out across the desert. "If it ever wakes again," she said quietly, "it won't find a reflection left to answer it."

They turned and began the long walk toward the horizon, leaving no footprints behind. The wind erased their path almost as soon as it formed, smoothing the sand until it was as if they had never been there.

But deep below, where glass met stone, a single hairline crack gleamed for an instant, and then vanished.

15

The desert had gone silent again. Not the kind of silence that followed a storm, but something deeper, older. The air itself felt hollow, emptied of vibration. Tara could hear her own breath inside her mask, slow and even, the only sound for miles.

The tomb was gone. The trench that had once led into the earth had filled itself, smooth and unbroken, as if the desert had grown tired of holding secrets.

Tara stood there, boots half buried, eyes fixed on the place where everything had happened. The morning light slanted low across the sand, soft and colorless. There was no trace of what lay beneath—no crack, no sound, not even the faint hum she'd grown used to feeling in her chest.

Behind her, the remains of the dig camp looked skeletal. Collapsed tents leaned at odd angles. Equipment lay half covered by sand. The main generator had died sometime during the night, leaving only the soft whine of the small solar battery powering their Starlink array.

Alex crouched beside the antenna, adjusting one of the panels. His hands were blistered and raw, but his movements were calm. "It's still online," he said, voice low but steady. "Signal's weak, but it's holding."

El-Amin sat a few feet away, his back against a broken support pole. The exhaustion in his face was etched deep, but his eyes were alert, tracking the horizon. "Good," he said. "When the sun's higher, it should stabilize. Then we can make the call."

Tara turned toward them. "And if it doesn't?"

Alex glanced up. "Then we walk. But I'd rather not test how far the next signal tower is."

She nodded faintly and looked back at the dunes. A breeze swept across the surface, carrying a whisper of movement. It sounded almost like breath. She closed her eyes and listened, half expecting to hear the faint harmonic again. Nothing came.

It was over. It had to be.

El-Amin rubbed his palms together, his voice barely more than a murmur. "The desert has taken it back. That much is certain."

"Do you think it's really gone?" Tara asked.

He considered the question before answering. "Gone isn't the right word. Contained, maybe. The resonance was never alive in the way we understand. It was memory trapped in a loop. Now that loop has closed."

Alex stood and brushed the sand from his hands. "If you're wrong, we'll know soon enough."

Tara smiled faintly, though it didn't reach her eyes. "You're an optimist."

"I'm tired," he said. "There's a difference."

The sunlight strengthened, turning the dunes from gray to gold. The antenna's indicator light blinked green. Alex gave a small nod. "We're online."

El-Amin reached into his pocket and pulled out his phone. The screen flickered to life, the signal bar faint but visible. "It's working."

Tara's pulse quickened. "Tommy?"

"Give me a second," El-Amin said. He opened the secure channel, the one they used for field operations. The satellite relay lagged, taking its time connecting to the outer network. Finally, the icon turned blue. "You're better at this," he said, handing her the phone.

She took it, thumb hovering over the call button for a moment before pressing it. The ring tone sounded distant and tinny, but it was there.

Three rings. Four.

Then, finally, a voice. "Watson?"

The sound of Tommy's voice almost broke her. "We're here," she said, keeping her tone steady. "We made it out."

"Oh, good," Tommy said. "I was beginning to worry. What happened?"

She glanced at Alex, then at El-Amin. Both were watching her closely. "The tomb collapsed. Completely. The chamber sealed itself. Whatever energy source was inside—it's gone."

"Gone how?" Tommy's tone sharpened slightly.

"Contained," she said. "That's the best word for it."

Tommy was silent for a long moment. When he spoke again, his voice had softened. "You three are still at the site?"

"Yes. The camp's mostly down, but we have power. The comms survived."

"Good," he said. "You'll stay put until we can get a containment team out there. I'll call in logistics tonight."

Alex stepped closer, speaking loud enough for the mic to pick him up. "Make sure they bring the right gear. This place isn't just unstable. It feels wrong."

Tommy's voice carried a touch of grim humor. "Coming from you, that means something."

"It means don't send rookies," Alex said.

"I won't."

Tara sank onto a crate beside the comms unit, the phone still pressed to her ear. The relief in her chest was fragile, edged with disbelief. "It's over, then?" she asked.

"Sounds like it," Tommy said. "You did what no one else could. I'll handle the rest."

The wind picked up again, rattling a loose flap of canvas somewhere behind her. Tara glanced toward the trench. The sand shifted slightly, just enough to catch the light. For an instant, it almost looked like something was breathing beneath it.

"Tommy," she said quietly. "Send them soon."

"They'll be there in forty-eight hours," he said. "Until then, sit tight. You've done enough."

She closed her eyes. "Copy that."

The line went quiet except for the faint hum of the satellite connection. Then Tommy's voice returned, softer this time. "And, Tara... I'm glad you made it out."

"Me too," she said.

When the call ended, she let the phone rest in her lap. The silence that followed was both familiar and heavy.

El-Amin looked at her. "He'll send them?"

"Yes," she said. "He'll send them."

Alex sat beside her, his gaze on the dunes. "Then all that's left is waiting."

The desert didn't argue. It simply breathed around them, calm and endless, as if it had been holding its breath all along.

The desert cooled quickly after sundown. The air lost its color and the dunes turned to gray waves under a thin blue sky. The camp lights flickered weakly, powered by what little charge the solar array had collected. Every sound carried too far—the soft creak of canvas, the faint grind of shifting sand, the brittle whisper of wind through the collapsed scaffolding.

Tara sat by the comms rig again, the small glow of her phone the only light near her. The call from earlier kept replaying in her head. Tommy's voice had steadied her then, but now it felt distant, like a half-remembered dream.

Across from her, Alex checked the truck's fuel gauge for the third time, though he already knew the reading. "We'll make it to the ridge when the containment crew gets here," he said. "If the batteries hold, we can even give them coordinates before they land."

El-Amin sat near the tent entrance, penlight between his fingers, sketching what he remembered of the chamber. The drawings were rough, almost abstract—the curve of the altar, the pattern of the mirrored plates, the way the resonance had folded inward. His hand trembled slightly.

Tara watched him for a while before speaking. "You're still writing it down?"

He didn't look up. "If I don't, I'll start to forget what it looked like."

"Maybe that's a good thing."

He stopped writing. The penlight made a faint circle on the page. "It might be," he said quietly. "But history has a way of punishing those who choose to forget."

The Starlink array pinged once. The sound was soft, but it cut through the quiet like a chime. Alex looked up. "Incoming?"

Tara checked her phone. The signal light blinked green again. "It's Tommy."

She accepted the call, putting it on speaker. The audio crackled for a moment before his voice came through, warm and calm. "Watson, Knox, El-Amin—you still in one piece?"

"Mostly," Alex said. "We're a little low on everything but dust."

"I'm not surprised," Tommy said. "You'll get some company soon. Containment team's already on the move. They'll reach you within thirty-six hours."

Tara felt the tightness in her chest ease. "That's sooner than expected."

"I called in every favor I had," he said. "The Agency's treating this as a Level Five lockdown. That site gets sealed, and then it disappears from every archive on record. The only people who'll remember it are the three of you and me."

El-Amin closed his notebook. "Good. It's not something anyone should try to wake again."

Tommy hesitated. "Is it stable?"

"Yes," Tara said. "Completely still. No vibration, no light. It's like it was never there."

"That's exactly how I want it to stay."

A pause followed. The sound of his breathing came through

faintly; slow and deliberate. When he spoke again, his tone was softer. "You did well, all of you. I mean that."

Alex leaned back against the supply crate. "We did what we had to do."

"Most people wouldn't have made it out," Tommy said. "Whatever was in that chamber, it would have taken anyone else with it. But you three stopped it. That's what matters now."

Tara looked out at the dunes. The moon was climbing higher, turning the sand silver. "Stopping it doesn't feel like winning."

"Maybe not," Tommy said. "But you bought us time. Sometimes that's enough."

El-Amin rubbed his temple. "What happens when they arrive?"

"They'll run sweeps, take seismic readings, and set charge anchors for permanent containment. After that, no one goes near that site again."

"And us?" Tara asked.

"You're finished there," he said. "When the containment crew gets to you, hand over the data logs and whatever equipment you've got left. Then you disappear for a while."

"Disappear?"

"Take time off," Tommy said. "All of you. You've been running for months, and this one nearly buried you. Go somewhere quiet. Ocean, mountains, I don't care. Just not another excavation."

Alex smiled faintly. "You're actually telling us to rest? You?"

Tommy's chuckle was low but genuine. "Even I know when to quit. I can tell from your voices you've been through hell. So consider this an order. Get clear of that site, get some air, and try to remember what normal feels like."

Tara leaned forward, her voice softer now. "And if the readings change? If the silence breaks?"

"Then you call me," he said. "But I don't think it will. The kind of silence you described doesn't come easy. It's earned."

The wind picked up outside the tent, brushing across the microphone. For a second, the static almost sounded alive, like something whispering between the words. Tara stared at the phone, her pulse quickening. Then the sound faded, leaving only the steady connection.

"You'll keep me posted?" she asked.

"I will," Tommy said. "But for now, Watson, get some sleep. You sound like you haven't closed your eyes in days."

"Feels longer than that."

He paused, as if considering his words carefully. "You did good," he said again, quieter this time. "Don't let what happened out there take that away from you."

The call ended with a soft click.

For a long time, no one spoke. The tent seemed smaller now, the silence thicker.

Finally Alex said, "He's right about one thing. I don't even remember the last time I slept."

El-Amin gave a tired laugh. "I'm not sure I remember what sleep feels like."

Tara set the phone down beside the comms rig. "Then maybe we should find out."

They extinguished the lantern and lay down in their cots, the faint glow of the Starlink unit casting a small pool of light against the canvas. Outside, the wind carried a steady rhythm, soft and patient, as if the desert were singing itself back to sleep.

Tara closed her eyes and listened. For once, there was no hum beneath her heartbeat. No echo. Just silence.

AFTERWORD

Thanks so much for reading this story. I hope you enjoyed it. If you did, check out more of Tara and Alex's adventures in the Paranormal Archaeology Series here: https://readerlinks.com/l/1053511

And be sure to subscribe to the VIP reader club to get a free story, character guides, exclusive concept art, and updates on the next project so you never miss out. Join here: https://readerlinks.com/l/3411801

I hope to see you in the next story.

Your friendly neighborhood author,

Ernest

ALSO BY ERNEST DEMPSEY

Sean Wyatt Adventures:

The Secret of the Stones

The Cleric's Vault

The Last Chamber

The Grecian Manifesto

The Norse Directive

Game of Shadows

The Jerusalem Creed

The Samurai Cipher

The Cairo Vendetta

The Uluru Code

The Excalibur Key

The Denali Deception

The Sahara Legacy

The Fourth Prophecy

The Templar Curse

The Forbidden Temple

The Omega Project

The Napoleon Affair

The Second Sign

The Milestone Protocol

Where Horizons End

Poseidon's Fury

The Florentine Pursuit

The Inventor's Tomb

ACKNOWLEDGMENTS

I'd like to give a big thanks to editors Anne Storer, and James Slater for their work on this story, as well as invaluable feedback from Allison Valentine.

I really appreciate the help.

www.ingramcontent.com/pod-product-compliance
Lightning Source LLC
Chambersburg PA
CBHW051959170626
46808CB00007B/2690